COOKED

THE LUCIE RIZZO MYSTERY SERIES

ADRIENNE GIORDANO

THE LUCIE RIZZO MYSTERY SERIES

Dog Collar Crime

Knocked Off

Limbo (novella)

Boosted

Whacked

Cooked

Romantic suspense books available by Adrienne Giordano

PRIVATE PROTECTOR SERIES

Risking Trust

Man Law

A Just Deception

Negotiating Point

Relentless Pursuit

Opposing Forces

HARLEQUIN INTRIGUES

The Prosecutor

The Defender

The Marshal

The Detective

The Rebel

JUSTIFIABLE CAUSE SERIES

The Chase

The Evasion

The Capture

CASINO FORTUNA SERIES

Deadly Odds

JUSTICE SERIES w/MISTY EVANS

Stealing Justice

Cheating Justice

Holiday Justice

Exposing Justice

Undercover Justice

Protecting Justice

Missing Justice

STEELE RIDGE SERIES w/KELSEY BROWNING

& TRACEY DEVLYN

Steele Ridge: The Beginning

Going Hard (Kelsey Browning)

Living Fast (Adrienne Giordano)

Loving Deep (Tracey Devlyn)

Breaking Free (Adrienne Giordano)

Roaming Wild (Tracey Devlyn)

Stripping Bare (Kelsey Browning)

Cooked: A Lucie Rizzo Mystery
Copyright © 2017 by Adrienne Giordano
(Original title Dog Collar Cuisine)
ISBN: 978-1-942504-21-4
Cover Art by Lewellen Designs
Editing by Gina Bernal

COOKED

A Lucie Rizzo Mystery
by
Adrienne Giordano

1

On a gray January day in Chicago, Lucie Rizzo shoved her shop's door closed, blocking out the frigid wind as Coco Barknell's potential future headed down the sidewalk. At her feet, Jimmy Two-Toes' mangy Jack Russell terrier, Sonny, licked his chops.

"Did you see this dog devour that food? Look at him. He'd sell his soul for another shot at that marinated chicken. We should jump on this."

Lucie's business partner and all-around BFF, Roseanne, sat at her desk, her sexy-librarian reading glasses perched on her nose.

"That dog," she said, eyes still on her monitor, "was a half-starved stray when Jimmy found him. He'd sell his soul for gruel. *Not* a good barometer."

The clunk of the furnace echoed through the large room that had once been Carlucci's shoe store. For years, Lucie's mom had bought their shoes in this very place. Now it housed Lucie's growing dog-walking and upscale pet accessory business.

Sonny doing that crazy leap as he followed her. She set the jar down and Sonny bounced up again.

"That jumping makes me nuts," Ro said.

"It's a Jack Russell thing. Jimmy said he can clear a five-foot fence."

Lucie glanced down at him and he bared his teeth. Smiling. At least Jimmy called it smiling. Lucie wasn't quite sure. Every time he did it though, Jimmy tossed him a piece of beef jerky. Whatever this teeth-baring thing was, the dog meant no harm. He was just jonesing for a treat.

She bent down and tickled him under the chin. "You're a scroungey looking thing, but you're cute."

He nudged his head toward the desk and shifted his eyes back to her.

"Look at him. Total man-slut for this food." She leaned in, offered up her cheek, and Sonny swiped his tongue over it. "Good boy. And since I'm a sucker, I'll give you the rest of this food. Just don't tell your daddy. You know he's watching your calories."

Ro pushed out of her chair, straightened her silk blouse, and did that strutting walk of hers to retrieve the bowl Sonny cleaned on his first round.

Before the remaining chicken and lamb hit the bowl, Sonny was in motion, shoving his snout right under Lucie's hand.

Ro stood by, tapping one stiletto clad foot. "I don't know, Luce. This scares me."

"Why?"

She gestured to the garment rack holding her latest design samples, all handmade for various sizes of dogs. Everything from Chihuahuas to Great Danes. "What we do, we can produce ourselves. We have a team of seamstresses that help us, yes, but it doesn't take a huge distribution plant. What you're talking about is a food product. The standards will be different. We'd have to partner with a large-scale processing plant. Which is exactly why Jo-Jo hasn't been able to grow this business. She said it herself."

"That's *not* what she said. The small factories can't handle the demand, but the bigger ones require more orders than she currently has. Without additional capital, she simply can't afford to expand. She's needs a backer. With my banking contacts, that's a problem I can fix—for a cut of the profits. It's a win-win."

Ro tossed her glasses on the desk and peered down at Sonny, who licked the bowl clean. "It's your company."

Really, it wasn't. Not anymore. The papers were still with the lawyer, but based on Ro's performance over the past year, Lucie had decided to give her BFF a fifteen percent share of Coco Barknell.

"Actually," Lucie said, "I need to talk to you about that."

"Uh-oh. I swear, Lucie Rizzo, if you tell me you've sold this company I will kill you where you stand. I will bury your body where it'll never be found."

Oh, the drama. As if.

Ro knew as well as anyone that Lucie's plan included Coco Barknell on the Fortune 500 list. Jo-Jo's Pride, and its innovative mix and match menu, might help get them there.

Lucie held up a hand. "Easy, killer. I'm not selling the company." *Not unless there are a lot of zeros in the number.* "But I am bringing on a partner who—"

Ro's jaw dropped. If Lucie knew her BFF at all, the jaw drop would be followed by a display of drama rivaled only by Broadway. And, yep...

She flapped her arms, sending her curvy body into

motion, boobs and hips—everything really—swinging. "A partner! Oh my God, you are *totally* killing me today. First the dog food and now a *partner*? I should resign right now. Forget the betrayal and walk away so we can still be friends."

Lucie laughed. Had to love Ro. "If you'd let me finish—"

"Who's this partner? Probably some big shot banker who will strip all the charm out of this thing."

Ro's voice carried a desperate vibration Lucie didn't hear all that often.

Tough, independent Roseanne was about to...cry. Lucie's stomach clenched into a hard knot. How had she blown this announcement so fiercely?

She put her hands up. "Stop. Please. It's not a banker. It's you, dopey! You're the partner."

Ro's head snapped back. "Wha?"

"You're the partner. You do so much for Coco Barknell. Way beyond an employee. Without your drive and designs, the accessory line would never have come this far. I thought you should have a stake in its future. I'm giving you fifteen percent of Coco Barknell. If we succeed, we succeed together."

"Come on. Really?" She stabbed a finger in Lucie's direction. "Don't you tease me."

Lucie laughed. "I'm not." She crossed her heart like they used to when they were ten years old, swearing each other to secrecy over their latest crushes. "Cross my heart."

Her BFF threw her arms around her and squeezed. "Lucie! That's...amazing." Her voice gave into the vibration and cracked. "I...can't believe it."

All that tough girl bluster and she was crying over being made a partner. God, Lucie loved her. They'd been perfect foils since childhood, and Lucie gave thanks each day for such a friendship.

"Well, believe it. We're partners now. So, if you really don't want to do this dog food deal, I'll reconsider it. But we should at least do the research. Let me talk to some folks and see if it's viable. That's all I'm asking. What do you say? Shall we take a shot?"

Ro backed away and held Lucie at arm's length. She tipped her chin up, wiped under her eyes—because God forbid a smudge dared to mar her perfect features. "Fine. But I'm going on record. If we wind up with a warehouse full of dog food, I'm not using my cleavage to sell it."

"Oh, ha-ha. Relax. All I'm doing is giving the idea it's due diligence. And I know exactly where to start."

———

THE THING LUCIE LOVED ABOUT OWNING HER OWN BUSINESS was the ability to commandeer a particular assignment when needed. Something her part-timer hardly minded since it gave her wiggle room in the packed daily schedule.

Which reminded Lucie she needed to hire another dog walker. Managing a growing business took precision—and a nagging brother who commented daily that they were on the cusp of a total dog-walking crisis.

Brie, the uppity Griffon Bruxellois owned by Chef Antoine Durand, paused in front of the famed Restaurant Durand to sniff a light pole.

While Brie did her thing, Lucie checked her watch. A sixty-five minute walk—on a windy day so cold that Lucie's nose hairs might be permanent ice sculptures. Even the rare appearance of the sun—thank you so much, Mother Nature —failed to bring the temperature up.

Chef's attention to time and schedules rivaled her own.

Antoine upstairs. He'd converted the apartment above the restaurant to an office suite and liked to hunker down with paperwork between the lunch and dinner rush.

Brie hopped up the stairs, tugging on the leash.

"Hold on, pushy."

Lucie unclipped her. This, Antoine had advised in the beginning, was their routine and Lucie wouldn't be the one to break it.

The dog disappeared through the open doorway at the top of the stairs and let out a yip.

"Hello, my girl," came Antoine's deep baritone.

Lucie could listen to that man talk all day. Ro helped with that by putting Antoine on speaker when he called the office. On a particularly slow day, she'd illegally recorded him via her cell phone and spent the afternoon replaying it over and over—and over—again, sighing and fanning herself while Lucie ate chocolate and giggled.

A couple of idiots.

She reached the top of the steps and hung a right into the short hallway. The first door led to Antoine's office. The adjacent bedrooms had been converted to a large conference room by knocking out a dividing wall. At the end of the hall was a small kitchen used mostly for coffee and soft-drinks rather than actual cooking.

Molly, Antoine's girlfriend-slash-manager leaned on the doorjamb to Antoine's office, her long honey-blond hair falling over one shoulder. She wore a V-neck purple dress under a matching coat and expertly applied makeup ala Ro. The few times Lucie had met Molly, she'd either been in casual clothes with minimal makeup or dressed to the hilt for a meeting. This was definitely the meeting look.

From what Lucie had heard, these two had broken up

and gotten back together enough to warrant mention on the local talk shows whenever it happened.

Having experienced the roller-coaster ride of breakups with her ex, Frankie, Lucie sympathized with the couple. Relationships were hard enough without the pressure of being a local celebrity. A handsome one to boot.

Thanks to Tim "O'Hottie" O'Brien, Lucie had left relationship drama behind. With Tim, she enjoyed plenty of laughter, good conversation, and a man who supported her without question. Where the relationship would go, she couldn't be sure. She didn't like to get too far ahead, but they'd exchanged the all-important I-love-yous *and* she kept a toothbrush at his house. Something Ro felt was akin to an on-the-horizon engagement ring.

Ro, though, was a little nuts and didn't have the greatest track record with men.

"Hi, Molly."

"Hi, Lucie. How are you?"

"Good, thanks. Just bringing Brie home."

"Hi, Lucie," Antoine called.

"Hi, Lucie," another female voice carried into the hallway.

Lucie poked her head in the doorway and waved at Molly's assistant, Annalise, and Antoine, who sat with Brie snuggled on his lap. Tiny Brie created an interesting contrast to Antoine's wide-shouldered, dark-featured intensity. The carved cheekbones didn't hurt his roguishly sexy looks.

Annalise returned the wave. "I'm glad you're here. Our apologies about that missing invoice. Something went fluky at the accountant's office."

As part of their management service, Molly and Annalise handled all invoices for Antoine. When the last

Coco Barknell payment hadn't arrived within thirty days, Lucie turned leg-breaker and called Annalise.

"It's not a problem. I assumed something went wacky."

Antoine sat at his desk, an oversized cherry deal with stacks of folders and papers strewn across the top. Two leather club chairs offered guest seating. Behind him was one of those giant safes that weighed more than an elephant. The safe door sat open, and Lucie pulled her gaze from it before Antoine thought her nosey.

"Thanks for handling that, Anna." Antoine turned to Lucie. "I thought Lauren would be here today."

Lucie handed him the leash, and he hung it on the hook behind his desk.

"She ran into a scheduling problem." *Liar, liar.* "I told her I'd handle Brie. And, by the way, she just peed on a woman out front."

Antoine fought a smile and nuzzled Brie. "Bad girl."

"Oh, Antoine," Molly said. "She's such a brat. This better not create one of those pain-in-the-ass frivolous lawsuits."

Lucie held up the business card the pee victim had given her. "Luckily, the woman is a groomer. She owns the shop down the street. She asked me to pass this along. I think she fell a little bit in love with your baby."

Antoine took the card and read it. "I guess since Brie defiled her, I should send her over for a bath." He lifted Brie and nuzzled her again. "Although Mr. Markus might be offended if I let someone else deal with that beard."

Annalise held out her hand. "Would you like me to make the appointment?"

"That'd be great. Thanks, Anna. And let's send her a casserole. Sucking up never hurts."

He set the dog back on his lap and looked at Lucie. "If you're hungry, stop in the kitchen and grab something."

"Oh, I'm fine. Thanks. If you have any of the casseroles made, I might grab one on my way out. My boyfriend is addicted."

"Good to hear. Keeps a roof over my head."

The simple recipe with beans, pork and sausage —*Cassoulet de Toulouse*, as the French called it—did more than keep a roof over Chef's head. After years of experimenting with his favorite recipe, he'd hit on a variation of ingredients that created a truly exceptional dish.

Now, three years later, in a flash of brilliance, he'd franchised the recipe, allowing other restaurants to pay for use of it. Only no one entity received the full ingredient list. From what Lucie knew, three food processing plants each received a list of herbs and spices they mixed and packaged. Then all three shipped the ingredients to customers, who mixed them and added the meat, beans, and breadcrumbs.

All of this wizardry made Antoine the most eligible billionaire in Chicago. Maybe the entire country.

Molly boosted off the doorframe and walked to Antoine. When she reached him, she pecked him on the lips. "Gotta go, doll. Call us if you have questions on those contracts."

Molly and Anna exited, but Lucie hovered in front of Antoine's desk. He continued to stroke Brie's back.

"Lucie, you look like you have something on your mind."

Ah, the perfect transition. "Actually, I do. Forgive me if this is too forward, but could I ask you something?"

His eyebrows hitched up. *Whoopsie.* Best to clarify. She held up her hands. "A *business* question."

He nudged his chin at the giant blue binder in front of him. "Of course. I'm working on payroll. I'll take any distraction."

"Thanks. I appreciate it. I've been approached by an

acquaintance with a business opportunity for Coco Barknell."

"Ah, my favorite thing."

He swiveled on his chair, set Brie on the faux fur doggie bed next to the floor safe.

"Take a nap," he said before turning back to Lucie. "I'm all yours. Tell me about this business opportunity. You're hesitant?"

"Actually, no. I'm the reverse. My partner is hesitant. It's a dog food line and Ro feels it's out of our wheelhouse."

"A dog food line. Interesting."

"Oh, it's more than that. It's...well...different."

"Different how?"

No matter how much she trusted Antoine, giving him the details of Jo-Jo's Pride without a confidentiality agreement in place was bad business. Bad business that shrewd women didn't partake in. Particularly when solid ideas could be swiped by seemingly trustworthy acquaintances.

"I'd love to tell you about it, obviously. But I've signed a non-disclosure agreement." She dug into her messenger bag for the blank agreement she'd brought with her. Just in case. No one would ever accuse her of not being prepared. "I was hoping you'd be willing to speak to me, so I brought a NDA with me."

He waggled a hand, took the document, perused and signed it. No muss, no fuss. Excellent.

She stowed it in her bag and prepared for take two of Land This Investor. "The dog food. It's basically a mix and match thing. Customers go to the website and choose beef, pork, chicken or lamb. Or, and this is what I love, the different proteins can be mixed. Maybe pork and chicken for one meal and then the next beef and lamb. Whatever.

The customer creates them, my client mixes the meals and delivers them."

"She's local then?"

"Yes. And she only delivers within a thirty-mile radius. She needs a better infrastructure for ordering. If I can get her some capital, we can expand, expand, expand. The food plants she works with now are too small to handle anything more."

Antoine nodded. "And the big guys won't touch her. I went through this with the casserole spices."

"Exactly."

He kicked back in his chair, propped his feet on the desk, and stacked his hands on his midsection. The king relaxing on his throne. "What kind of numbers is this business pulling?"

"She's been operating eighteen months and has $99,500 in revenue."

Chef's bottom lip rolled out. "That's not bad. You're looking for an investor then?"

"To do what I think the business needs, yes. I don't have that kind of capital and to compete in an already crowded market, she'll need to expand the food choices and ship nationwide. I have contacts from my banking days, but I'm wondering, based on your experience with food manufacturers, if you thought this would be a viable business. Is a successful expansion even possible?"

He tilted his head one way, then the other. "If you can get the ordering system in place and the processing plants on board, it sounds solid. And it's different. You have a business plan?"

"Not yet. I'll write one up." She smiled. "This is my feeling-it-out phase."

"Well, it's intriguing. At least to me. Would you be open to making me a partner?"

Cha. Ching! A partner. Walking in here, she'd intended only to ask his advice, but smart girls always left options open. In the back of her mind she'd hoped he—and his billionaire bank account—might have an interest in seeing his name on a dog food container. "Really?"

His Hotness gifted her with a crooked smile that sharpened the angles of his face. "You may have noticed, I'm famous. With that comes responsibility. I choose my endorsement deals carefully. I'm building a brand and won't slap my name on inferior products. Anything with food has to be quality. If you'll allow me to work with the plants on quality control, I'll throw in the capital and let you put my name on it."

"In exchange for what percentage?"

He smiled again. Nice try pal. Underneath her jeans and puffy coat was a killer. A financial shark. If he thought that smile would charm her into giving away money, he didn't know Joe Rizzo's kid at all.

"Sixty percent," he said. "And that's assuming you and this other partner will run everything and not take a salary until we're profitable."

She'd expected the no-salary demand and the higher percentage. Venture capital deals tended to carry those. Plus, he'd be throwing his name—and the marketing benefits of said name—on the product.

Still, sixty percent? Lucie let out a low whistle. "Can't do it. We're already bringing a following and, as you said, it's different. This isn't your run-of-the-mill dog food. Forty-nine percent."

"Fifty-five."

"That gives you controlling interest. Jo-Jo won't go for

that. And if I'm bringing this under the Coco Barknell umbrella, I'm not going for it either. How about fifty percent? That'll make you an equal partner."

Shouts sounded from below. Antoine cocked his head toward the door. A second later, a loud, blaring alarm went off.

"Chef!" Someone yelled from downstairs. "Fire!"

Brie let out three fast barks. Antoine hopped from his chair and peered down at her. "Shit."

"Go," Lucie said. "I'll get Brie."

2

LUCIE CORNERED THE DESK, ALREADY REACHING FOR THE HOOK holding Brie's leash. Of all the ways to die, a fire would be one of the worst. Too unpredictable. And deadly. One second you had a candle lit and the next, the whole place was up in flames. Flames that stole precious oxygen.

Already the smell of smoke drifted upstairs.

Hurry.

Her pulse slammed as she snapped the leash on Brie, who let out three yips. Dogs were smart that way. They sensed danger. The best Lucie could do was keep her own emotions under control and not send the pup into a panic.

"I know, girl. We'll be fine. Let's just get out of here."

She scooped her up and made her way to the top of the stairwell. A blast of heat roared upward. At the bottom, the kitchen staff rushed out, each of them pushing at the person in front, urging them to move faster.

"Move," one man said, "before it spreads and we're all toast."

Brie yipped again, drawing the attention of one of the servers.

"No!" The guy said. "Take her out the back. If they don't get the fire out fast, the whole place will be engulfed."

Again, Brie yipped, her tiny body shivering.

Lucie swung around, staring straight down the hallway to the back door. By the time she got there, she could be down these steps and out.

"Close that door," someone yelled from below.

The server, now almost to the exit, turned back and… froze. "Holy shit," he said.

Lucie saw it, the flick of bright orange that shot around the doorframe then retreated. Flick, retreat, flick, retreat.

Flames.

Right there.

Get out.

Forget not panicking. A rush of energy consumed her. Made her skin tingle. She spun, charged down the hall, her feet heavy on the hardwood. Brie shivered and yipped again and Lucie forced a cooing noise, but Brie wasn't having it. She let out another yip, her tiny paws scrabbling for purchase in Lucie's arms.

"It's okay, girl. We're fine. Just need to get you out the other door."

They passed Antoine's office, reaching the small galley kitchen and the door that led to the fire escape.

"Lucie!"

Antoine's voice. From below.

"We're going out the back. I've got her. We'll meet you out front."

Lucie reached down, gripped the doorknob.

Locked. She lifted her hand, now trembling from the adrenaline overload and…oh no. A double-key lock.

Trapped.

Before today, she'd considered a key to unlock the door from either side pure genius. Excellent safety measure.

Except during a fire.

"Antoine," she screamed, sending Brie into another yip-fest. "Where's the key?"

No answer from Antoine.

Lucie scanned the countertops. No keys. The walls. Nothing. "I'm going to fry in this place."

No sir. Not happening.

Think.

A small squeak left her throat and Brie's paws got active again, the dog struggling to break free.

Don't panic. "Easy, girl. We're okay."

Hanging on to Brie with one arm, Lucie went to work flinging open the few cabinets. No keys. She inhaled, felt the burn of smoke in her throat.

It's coming.

Drawers. She yanked on them. Nothing. Cabinet below the sink. Only place left. She whipped open the door and... there! Hanging on a small hook on the inside of the door. A key.

Ripping it off the hook, she fumbled it, trying to right it with her free hand. Between rushing and her trembling fingers...whoopsie...she dropped it.

"Damn it."

She set Brie down and concentrated on swiping the key off the floor. Her first attempt at sliding it into the lock failed. Of course. She steadied herself, breathed deep, and tried again.

Another burst of energy erupted, this one a surge of relief that settled her hammering pulse.

She yanked open the door, welcoming the chill of winter and the fresh air that came with it. Bending low, she scooped up Brie. "We've got this, girlfriend. Let's get out of here."

THREE FIRE EXTINGUISHERS AND THE BUILT-IN KITCHEN sprinklers did part of the job. The fire department did the rest. At least that's what Lucie had heard from some of the kitchen staff milling about with her.

She stood out of the way on the opposite corner while the firefighters dealt with the aftermath and made sure no secondary fires erupted. Brie played at her feet, happily flirting with passersby

A dog's life. So simple.

Across the street, Antoine talked with a cop, gesturing with his hands and looking around. He spotted her, waved, and in the distance, she saw it. The collapse of his shoulders as relief took hold. He finished with the cop and dodged traffic, totally jaywalking. Right in front of Chicago's finest. If she'd done that, they'd lock her up for ten years. But that's how her luck ran.

The light turned red and Antoine scooted around a car, earning himself a flip of the bird. At which point he returned the gesture, his passion obvious when he added the other hand. The dreaded double flip.

He shoved his hands through his dark hair, pushing it away from his face before he scooped up Brie for a nuzzle. "Lucie, thank you for staying with her. I'll pay you for the time."

"No problem. You don't have to pay me. I was glad to help. Besides, I ate up some of your time asking advice, so we're even. How's the kitchen?"

He glanced back at the building, his eyes more than a

little sad. "The fire is out, but it's a mess. I need to get a contractor in there and figure out how long we'll be shut down."

"What happened?"

"Grease fire. It spread so fast, by the time we got to the extinguishers half the kitchen was engulfed."

As if sensing his heartache, Brie craned her neck and licked Antoine's chin. "Thank you, baby," he said.

Lucie glanced back at the building, imagining the revenue loss, and hoped he had good insurance.

"Thanks again, Lucie. I should get back over there."

"Of course. Are you sure you want to take Brie? I'm heading home, but I could take her with me and when you're wrapped up here, you can come get her. Or I can have my boyfriend bring her back tonight when he goes home. Either way."

Antoine looked over at the restaurant again, twisted his lips one way then the other. "She really shouldn't be in that building right now. Would you mind?"

If it kept the dog safe, she'd do it. Sweet girl could step on debris or suffer smoke inhalation. Plus, if Lucie's help got him to invest in the dog food venture, she'd consider it a bonus. Did that make her a horrible person? Probably. But a girl had to make a living.

"Not at all. She's good company."

Lucie held her hands out. "Come on, you little bugger. Let's go see what the lunatics at Villa Rizzo are doing."

———

AT 6:05, LUCIE RUSHED THROUGH THE FRONT DOOR OF VILLA Rizzo with Brie happily yipping at her feet. Leave it to a dog to think it was all fun and games.

Beyond the living room, her family cluttered around the dining table. Joey sat in his usual spot at the end with Ro to his right next to Mom. Tim, patient and hopefully understanding, occupied the adjacent seat.

Lucie shut the door, tripped over the dog, and fell ass over elbow. *Oh, no.* On her way to the floor, she cruised by the bannister and made a useless attempt to grab hold. Missed. *Dang it.* She landed on her butt, the pain radiating straight up her spine.

"Ow! Shit."

"Language," Mom said from the table.

Brie, assuming it was play time, pounced, giving Lucie a massive face lick.

Dear God. What an entrance. "Off, Brie. Off!"

Tim hopped up just as Joey spun around to see what the racket was. "What the hell? Tryin' to eat here. Why is the Ewok here?"

Lucie shoved a hand in front of Brie's mouth to stop the onslaught of wet tongue. "That's okay, Joey. I'm not hurt or anything. You jerk."

Tim strode up, grabbed the dog, holding her in one hand while helping Lucie up with the other.

Those hands. They created miracles in the world of Lucie Rizzo.

And how awesome was it having a hunky alpha to take care of her?

She smiled up at him, looking handsome in his rolled-up shirt-sleeves and open collar. A few wisps of strawberry-blond chest hair poked out of the open button. Lucie's mind went naughty places. How she loved her red-headed detective. "Thank you."

"You okay?"

With him around? Perfect. "I'm fine."

"What's that animal?" Dad hollered from the table. "I don't want animals in here."

Meeting Tim's gaze, Lucie grunted. "I'm so sorry I left you alone with the lunatics. The Kennedy was a parking lot. As usual. I swear they should bomb that thing."

"No big deal. We watched SportsCenter." He leaned in close to her ear. "And I got career advice from your Dad, who advised me to stay away from certain Area 3 cops. He thinks they're dirty."

That warning coming from Joe Rizzo, mob boss? Priceless.

Brie stared up at Tim then launched herself up in an attempt to sneak a lick of his chin. Lucie couldn't blame her. She often felt that way around him. Ro didn't call him O'Hottie for nothing.

Tim, apparently unable to resist the cuteness, scratched the underside of the dog's chin. "Luce? Is this really a dog?"

Joey waved a fork. "It's the Ewok."

Lucie rolled her eyes. "Shut up with the Ewok jokes. She's a *Griffon*. It's a rare breed. You should have a little respect."

"Lucia," Mom said, "stop this nonsense and come eat before it gets cold. Wash your hands."

Second grade. That's what living here felt like. "Yes, ma'am."

Joey caught her eye as they wandered by. "I'll ask again. Why do you have the Ewok?"

If her brother made it to thirty without Lucie burying him at a SuperFund site, it would be a miracle. The toxicity alone would make him disintegrate. When it came to being annoying, he'd settled down some since he'd started dating Ro. But, he had a ways to go yet before Lucie might consider him human. Total work-in-progress.

While Tim held Brie, Lucie unclipped the leash and wished they had more doors on the first floor to contain pee-girl. Better to keep her in sight. "I went to see Antoine."

"The casserole guy?"

"Yep. I walked Brie for Lauren today. When I brought her back, a fire broke out at the restaurant."

"Oh, my goodness," Mom said. "Was anyone hurt?"

"No. It was a kitchen fire. They put it out, but I told Antoine I'd keep Brie while he dealt with the mess."

"You're such a good girl, Lucie," Mom said. "Always right there to help."

Dad nodded his agreement without disturbing a single hair on his perfectly groomed salt-and-pepper hair. "We did good with her."

"Really, Joe? *We*?"

Tim cleared his throat and nudged Lucie along. Alrighty then. No need to get into the deets on Dad's absence during Joey and Lucie's formative years.

Before the debate broke out, Lucie marched into the kitchen. "I was in the middle of negotiating with him to be an investor in the dog food deal, so it wasn't totally altruistic." She gestured at Brie still in Tim's hand. "You can put her down."

Tim set her on the floor and she sniffed her way around the room. If this dog peed in here, Lucie would never hear the end of it.

After washing their hands, they took their places at the dining room table.

Joey cocked his head. "You met with Jo-Jo this morning?"

"We did," Ro said. "Your sister is all fired up about this dog food deal."

Lucie handed the bowl of potatoes off to Tim and watched him shovel a mountain of them onto his plate.

to make Lucie's heart pound. "Whatever you're about to say, stop. With that lead in, it can't be good and then I'll have to stab you in the eye."

"I didn't hear that," Tim cracked.

"She's not pregnant," Lucie said, hoping it was true. Joey was right. The weight gain couldn't be denied. "You people are insane. The big news is I made her a partner in the business."

Lucie's phone rang and she shoved out of her chair to retrieve it from her messenger bag. "Sorry. This might be Antoine looking for his dog."

"Let's hope," Dad said. "I don't like animals in here. So," he turned to Ro, "you're a partner now. That's good. Congratulations."

After retrieving the phone, Lucie jabbed at the screen, barely catching the call before it went to voicemail. "Antoine, hi. That was fast. Are you done already?"

"No. Not yet. I'm in my office though."

His voice sounded funny. Raspy and...rushed. Probably the stress of the day. "Is everything okay?"

"When you grabbed the leash off the hook did you see a blue card anywhere? Maybe on the floor?"

A blue card? She thought back, but the only thing she'd noted was the binder. And the open safe. "Not that I remember. Why?"

"The card is my casserole recipe. I keep a hard copy in the safe."

"Oh."

"Yeah. *Oh*."

His recipe. The world-famous one that made him a billionaire. The *secret* recipe with more security than a nuclear facility. A sizzling panic shot up Lucie's neck. "Are you sure it's not there. Maybe it's under something?"

"I tore the whole place apart. It's not here. *Someone* took it."

3

Someone, meaning Lucie?

Come on! Seriously? After helping him with the dog he thought...

"Antoine, I hope you don't think it was me."

From the other room, Tim shifted in his seat, his entire body now facing her.

"All I know is it's gone."

"Well, don't panic. I'll bring Brie back and help you look."

Before Antoine could respond, she hung up. If he thought he'd accuse her of stealing and not give her an opportunity to face him, he'd have to think again. Lucie Rizzo, mob princess, had dealt with people thinking less of her for too long to let that go unaddressed.

She stowed the phone in her messenger bag and headed back to the dining room.

Tim's hyper-focused green eyes unnerved her and gave panic a new life. "What's up?"

Lucie picked up her barely touched plate of food. "He can't find the casserole recipe. I told him I'd help him look."

From across the table, Mom huffed. "Now? First you were late and now you're leaving?"

"Mom, I'm sorry. I have to go."

"It's a recipe. You'd think it was fine art."

"In a way," Tim said, "it is. He's built an empire on that casserole." He glanced up at Lucie. "I thought he had CIA-proof security?"

"Yeah," Joey said, "He's always going on about how it's stored in a vault that has both eye and palm scanners."

"I guess he keeps a hard copy in his safe as well. It's one of those giant ones that weighs a bazillion pounds. The safe was open when I was in the office. Then the fire alarm went off and he ran."

Dad slapped a hand on the table sending the plates bouncing. "That son of a bitch thinks you *stole* it?"

Great. All she needed was Joe Rizzo getting his shorts in a wad. "No, Dad." *Liar.* "He's only asking if I saw it. I have to bring the dog back anyway, so I'll go there and help him look."

Tim stood. "I'll come with you."

"Good," Dad said. "If this guy thinks he's gonna accuse my baby girl, I want a detective there with her."

"Luce," Joey said, "this better not be another one of your screwy situations. I'm maxed out on those."

And she wasn't?

———

TIM SPENT THE RIDE DOWNTOWN GRILLING LUCIE ON THE details of her meeting with the chef. As a detective, he'd learned not to overlook seemingly inconsequential facts. Even the minute ones, like where the dog was when all this

Maybe we should mash one of them and see if there's anything in the middle?"

Bile backed up in his throat. Gag reflex. The day job exposed him to a lot. Blood, wounded animals, torn flesh. All of that, he could handle.

The smell of dog shit? Killed him. Every time. He straightened up, shoved his shoulders back, and inhaled the moist lake air until his stomach settled down.

From her bent position, Lucie looked up at him. "Oh, come on. The big bad detective can't handle dog poop?"

"It's the smell."

"Once again, it takes a woman."

At that, Tim laughed. "Normally, I'd say go right ahead, but it might be evidence. Keep it intact."

Using the baggie, Lucie scooped up one of the samples and analyzed it, rolling it around in her hand.

Tim gagged again and took three steps back. "Ack. That's so nasty."

"My hero."

"Wait till we're done here and I'll show you a hero."

That put a smile on her face. And he hadn't even touched her yet. One thing about Lucie, she never hesitated when it came to them dropping their clothes.

"I'll look forward to that, Detective." She stood tall, tying the baggie and holding it up for his perusal. "I didn't see anything unusual. If Brie ate that card, it hasn't processed yet."

Processed. Good one. "How long does it usually take?"

Lucie shrugged. "It depends on the dog. Raw food can take four to six hours. Kibble might take ten to twelve. I have no clue about paper."

"We'll have to monitor that. Get Chef Ramsay to watch it."

Lucie smacked his arm. "Don't call him that. You might slip in front of him."

When Lucie had first landed Antoine as a client, Tim had jokingly referred to him as Chef Ramsay, the famous television chef. The name had stuck and Tim was having trouble breaking himself of it.

They reached the side entrance of the restaurant. Brie let out a yip.

"I know, sweetie. You missed Daddy."

Tim fought an eye roll as he opened the door. "When we're inside, stay calm. Don't let this guy rattle you."

"I'm not a drama queen—"

"I'm not saying you are."

"Then what are you saying?"

He popped a kiss on her lips. "You have a hot button when it comes to people making assumptions about your character."

"A hard-earned hot button. I've been judged my whole life."

"I know. Which is why you can't get emotional. I'll take the pressure off by telling him I'm a detective."

Lucie glanced inside at the staircase leading to the second floor. "Don't make it sound official. That'll spook him."

"It'll be a side note." He grinned. "Right before I search the place."

Sometimes a detective boyfriend made for nice perks. Like now when someone was about to accuse Lucie of theft.

Brie darted through the door, tugging on her leash, and Lucie followed her inside as the acrid odor of charred wood and dampness assaulted her senses. To her left, the door to the kitchen stood open. Lucie peeped in, spotted the black soot marring the previously pristine walls and various pots and oversized frying pans still standing on the stove. The roar from industrial fans tasked with drying puddles of standing water drowned out any possible noise. She shook her head. What a mess.

Behind her, Tim poked his head in the open doorway and once again shined his phone light.

He let out a low whistle and, rather than shout over the noise, bent close to her ear. "Amazing the damage fire can do in a short time."

"How long do you think this will take to clean up?"

"By the time they get the equipment repaired and inspections done? Probably two weeks."

Two weeks. "Ugh."

The hallway light flashed on. Antoine stood at the top of the stairs in a chef's coat with enough wrinkles to keep his dry cleaner in business for a lifetime. Wisps of his normally neat hair stuck up in all directions on either side of his head. *Not good.* The coat, the hair, all of it so out of character for the A-list chef.

"Hi, Antoine." She set her hand on Tim's bicep. "This is Tim O'Brien. My boyfriend."

The chef gave a terse nod. Clearly not a happy camper, but after the day he'd had, he was entitled to be crabby. As long as he didn't accuse her of being a thief, she'd give him a little leeway.

"Come up," he said. "Please lock that door behind you. I thought I locked it."

While Tim dealt with the lock, Lucie unclipped the leash. Brie shot up the stairs into her owner's arms. The love of a good dog. Some days, that's all people needed.

Antoine nuzzled Brie. His mouth moved, but between the distance and noise from the fans, Lucie couldn't make out the words. Probably just as well. Private moment and all that.

Antoine kept his gaze pinned to her as she made her way up the creaking wood stairs. The tension squeezed like a vise. Behind her, Tim tugged gently on the back of her jacket and she glanced back. Her red-headed hunk gave her a thumbs up. She nodded, understanding the silent support. Lordy, how did she deserve this man?

When Antoine refused to step back and make room for them, Lucie halted at the top of the stairs. "Any luck on the recipe?"

"No. I've torn that office apart."

Well, she'd have to help him look. Ignoring his attempt to block her from entering, Lucie inserted herself in the small space between Antoine and the doorframe. At certain times, her diminutive stature came in handy.

Tim, ever the professional, held his hand out. "Tim O'Brien. I'm a detective with Chicago PD. Thought I'd come along to help."

Antoine set Brie on the floor. She scampered off, probably in search of her bed after all the excitement of a road trip.

The two men shook hands. "Antoine Durand." He turned away from Tim, absently waving one hand. "Close that door behind you. I don't want Brie down there."

He led them to his office and once inside squatted to give Brie a rub while Tim scanned the space.

He lingered on the now-closed safe for a few seconds, head cocked. "Do you remember seeing the recipe? It's a blue card, yes?"

"I didn't take it out of the safe. It stays on the top shelf. I keep a notebook on that shelf too. I took the notebook out, but I didn't see the card fall out."

"Could the dog have swiped it?"

"Doubtful. She doesn't usually go for paper."

Lucie held up the poop bag she'd brought in with her. "We checked Brie's poop. I didn't see remnants of the card."

Tim glanced around the office again. "Have you checked the other rooms? Just in case."

"I looked." He lifted one hand to his forehead then dropped it. "I'm telling you, paper goods aren't an issue with her. You said you're a detective?"

Tim nodded. "Property crimes."

"How very *convenient*."

Now he wanted to be a smart ass. As if Lucie planned on stealing his stupid recipe and then having her detective boyfriend investigate. Wouldn't that make her an excellent criminal?

She held up her hands. "Let's be honest here. You think I stole that recipe."

Antoine stayed silent. Of course he did. A lifetime of being Joe Rizzo's kid had conditioned her to the silence that came with being judged.

"*Well*," she said, "I didn't. I may have been alone up here —trapped, I might add—while I searched for the damned door key, but, hey, you don't have to *thank* me for *saving* your *dog*. Instead, you can accuse me of being a thief."

Tim touched her forearm, probably to shut her up, but... no. Staying calm was one thing. She could do that, but she wouldn't stand around and be accused of a crime without spouting off a little.

"Luce—"

"No, Tim. I don't like being called a thief."

Antoine hit her with a hard look. "That card was in the

safe when the fire broke out. The door was open when I walked out and now the card is gone. It's not rocket science."

Oh, she should just smack that smug look off his face. Pompous idiot. Lucie curled her fingers, let her nails dig into the soft flesh of her palm and considered popping him. *Bam!* One good sock to the kisser.

But violence wasn't her thing. Aside from those few instances where she'd jumped on people. And maybe whacked them on the head a few times. Those were isolated instances and she was, in fact, a weakling who could hardly inflict any damage.

Right now, though? She could cut a bitch.

Tim stepped into the space separating Lucie and Antoine. "Let's stay focused. The three of us will search this floor, room by room. *Together.*"

"Fine." Antoine headed for the door.

"Fine," Lucie repeated, following the chef.

Tim sighed. "Fine."

———

FORTY-FIVE MINUTES AND THREE ROOMS LATER, LUCIE, TIM, and Antoine stood in the conference room after having completed their search.

No blue card anywhere.

"That," Antoine said, "was an epic failure."

Mr. Positive. Lucie gritted her teeth. *Ignore him.* That's all she'd do. For close to an hour she'd been listening to him either A) sigh or B) make some sort of passive aggressive remark aimed at her, the suspected recipe thief.

Visions of pummeling her client, just leaping on top of him and hammering away, filled Lucie's mind. *Not worth the jail time.*

Tim scratched the side of his face. To the untrained, the gesture appeared casual. Not to Lucie. For months, she'd studied this man's body language and learned his tells, even the ones hiding behind a mask of neutrality. That face scratch? Big trouble.

O'Hottie was worried.

Tim walked to the conference room door and pointed at the office across the hall. "When you opened the safe, do you remember seeing the card? I know you said you keep it on the top shelf, but are you sure you actually saw it today?"

"I'm positive. It was on top of the binder and I had to move it."

Don't panic.

Lucie took a lesson from Tim and kept her body language to a minimum. No disgusted outrage or arm flapping. Just...nothing.

"What about other people? Was anyone else up here after you opened the safe?"

"Only Molly and Annalise."

"And they are?"

"Molly is my girlfriend."

"And his manager," Lucie added. "Annalise is her assistant."

Apparently she'd forgotten to mention Molly and Anna to Tim, because he eyed her with the classic WTF look.

"Hey," she said, "it's been a rough day."

"Could either one of them have taken it?"

Antoine propped his hands on his hips and dipped his head back. "No. They weren't anywhere near the safe. Molly doesn't even know I keep a copy in there. She's the security freak. If she knew I kept a hard copy, she'd lecture me until I turned to stone."

Based on their current situation, she'd be right on with

that lecture. If anything, he shouldn't make a habit—even if in his office—of leaving the safe hanging open. Anything could happen. As evidenced by the kitchen fire.

"I understand," Tim said. "Was there anyone else up here?"

"Not while the safe was open."

Damn it.

The intercom buzzer sounded. Antoine strode back to his office with Lucie and Tim falling in behind. He punched a button on the keypad near his desk. "Hello?"

"Uh, hi." A voice boomed through the speaker. "I have a delivery for...uh...it says Antoine Durand."

"What kind of delivery?"

"An envelope."

Antoine shook his head as if it was the messenger's fault he'd had a crappy day.

Lucie and Tim waited in the hallway while Antoine signed for the envelope. The creak of stairs alerted them to Antoine's return, but then...silence.

"Son of a bitch!"

Tim charged toward the stairway with Lucie on his heels.

"What is it?"

In the middle of the staircase, Antoine held up a type-written sheet of paper. "It's a note. Telling me to await instructions and not call the cops if I don't want my recipe released. It appears I'm about to be blackmailed."

4

———

IN A GIANT BURST OF ENERGY, TIM TOOK OFF, HIS BIG BODY hustling down the stairs. He shoved Antoine aside, moving around him to get to the street level. Lucie fell in behind. Wherever her man went, she went too. Especially if it meant a chance to see the creep trying to frame her.

The second-floor entry door slammed behind her and she gripped the railing, taking a peek over her shoulder. Antoine had closed the door, locking Brie inside.

Tim leaped from the third step and whipped the outside door open. Wicked cold bit against her cheeks and her breath came in a white puff. *Oooff!* She slammed into the back of Tim and—*oooff* again!—got pancaked by Antoine who couldn't stop in time.

"Hey, Detective," Lucie said. "A little warning would be nice."

"Woo-hoo!"

Oh, no.

Behind her, Ro furiously waved one hand and strutted toward them, her high-heeled boots clickety-clacking against the pavement. What the heck was she doing here?

Antoine pointed to the far end of the block. "There he is. Red hat. On the corner."

Tim took off running, his suit coat flapping open as he moved, dodging the few pedestrians. Lucie fell in behind, her short legs failing to give her enough speed to keep up.

Antoine cruised by. Clearly, he went to the gym. Probably with Tim.

"Woo-hoo," Ro said again. "Wait for me."

No waiting. Lucie pumped her legs harder, sucking in long, slow breaths. These men wouldn't leave her behind. No way. Cold air singed her throat. Whoopsie. Should have grabbed her coat, because the sweater wouldn't cut it against the bitter lake air. She kept running though, willing her legs to go faster. Faster, faster, faster. Just to stay with them.

Ro tromped up behind her doing a weird waddle/walk/run. Even Ro, wearing sky high heels and a skirt that could double as plastic wrap, was faster than Lucie. They jockeyed around a woman pushing a stroller and managed to bump a guy carrying a briefcase.

"Sorry, handsome," Ro said.

"Anytime, hon."

Men. Total pigs.

"Luce," Ro huffed, "who are we chasing?"

"That guy just delivered a blackmail letter."

"Ooh, nice."

Lucie kept running, but with Ro distracting her, the men started pulling away. "We have to keep up. What are you doing here?"

"I was bored."

Bored. Excellent. "Where's Joey?"

"Please. Doing collections. Don't get me going on *that*."

And—oy—a side stitch shredded Lucie's torso. Her

heart slammed so hard her chest wall should have cracked open.

Gotta get to the gym.

The red hat guy spotted Antoine—not exactly incognito in his chef's coat— and darted into the street. Car tires screeched and a horn sounded, but the guy managed to not become road kill in the late rush hour traffic.

Tim jockeyed around the vehicles littering the intersection and disappeared from Lucie's view. Taking advantage of the stopped traffic, she scooted across both lanes and hooked a left, following but losing ground on Tim and Antoine.

God, she was out of shape.

The sidewalk edges blurred and she blinked, sucked more air and blinked again. Her chest hurt. Her side hurt. *Everything* hurt. Ahead, now more than half a block up, an overhead streetlight shined against Tim's hair. That cross between red and strawberry blond that she'd know anywhere.

Another horn sounded and she peered right, into the street where red hat guy whipped between cars and almost got flattened again.

Idiot. For that alone she wanted to catch him. He could have caused an accident. Killed someone. Not to mention himself.

And, right now, she might want that honor.

"Dumbass," a woman yelled. "Get out of the street."

My thoughts exactly.

Once again taking advantage of the stopped traffic, Lucie and Ro tore across the street and hopped onto the sidewalk in front of a lingerie boutique that had just turned its lights off, leaving them in the shadow of the street lamps.

She slowed her run—thank you, sweet baby Jesus—to a

speed walk, and forced out an even breath as her heart slammed and slammed. *Relax.*

Ro stopped in front of the lingerie store and poked at the shop's window. "Joey would love that bra."

"Hey! If you're going to be here, focus. We need to catch this guy."

Red hat guy stopped for a second, looking left at the sidewalk that was barricaded due to construction.

Got him. *You are toast, pal.*

He turned right. Running straight at Lucie and Ro.

What the hell?

Tim and Antoine followed, the guy now dead center between Lucie and the men. And he kept coming. Sure, she was small, but did he not see her?

She'd have to tackle him. Head on.

She glanced behind the guy, saw Tim gaining on him. Slow him down. That's all she had to do. A few steps and Tim would be on him.

She tugged on Ro's sleeve. "Help me slow him down. The guy with the red hat."

Prying herself from the slutty bra display, Ro did that funky waddle/speed walk and fell into step beside Lucie.

"You got it, sister."

"Tackle him if we have to, but make sure he doesn't get through. Tim is right behind him."

"I can flash him."

"No!"

All Lucie needed was Tim seeing Ro's boobs. With that, she'd lose him forever.

She shook off visions of Tim mesmerized by the beautiful Roseanne and focused on red hat guy. He had some bulk. Not nearly as tall as Tim, but enough where he'd do some damage if he ran head-on into Lucie. Ro maybe could take him. Lucie? No way.

Which left her with a decision. Cracked skull or being labeled a blackmailer?

Hmmm...

Cracked skull.

Definitely.

Now twenty feet away, she picked up speed, kept her eyes straight ahead, tracking her prey. He moved right to angle around a pedestrian and bumped another woman.

"Hey. Slow down. Jerk!"

Tell him, lady.

And then he was right there. No pedestrians blocking her view. Just her and red hat guy. He made a move, dodging left, but she picked up speed, running straight for him.

His eyes grew wide. Anticipating the crash, she let out a wail, an absolute war cry that was half pissed-off Italian girl and half let-me-live, and...leaped. Arms extended, she flew right at him.

"Luce," Tim said. "No!"

Halting, the guy put his hands up, twisting his upper body to block the blow. Too late.

She crashed into him, her peanut body barreling into his solid bulk. *Yow.* Her chest caved in. Or maybe her lungs split open, because she suddenly couldn't breathe.

The guy stumbled back. Ro appeared, swinging her giant Gucci purse and landing a paralyzing blow to the side of his head while Lucie fought for a decent breath, her lungs slowly filling and releasing.

"Ow," he said.

He kept moving, though, shoving at Lucie, who wrapped her arms around him. He dragged her along, the toes of her new shoes scraping against the pavement.

Her fingers slipped and she tightened her hold. "Watch the shoes. I just bought these."

Behind red hat guy, Tim came to a halt, grabbing the back of his jacket. "Luce. Off!"

Smack.

Ro walloped him again.

Tim angled away, avoiding the purse's rebound. "Watch it," he said. "You almost got me."

Antoine joined the crowd, adding reinforcement. Lucie, still hanging from the much bigger guy's shoulders, let go. She dropped to the pavement, her knees taking a direct hit.

"Ouch."

"You okay?"

She gave Red Hat her mean face. "I'm fine. No thanks to this jerk." She shook a fist at him. "You could have gotten us killed!"

Tim slid between her and Red Hat.

"Antoine, is this him? The guy who delivered the letter?"

Antoine rested his hands on his thighs and bent over, drawing hard inhalations. "That's him. Now I want some answers."

THE SOUND OF SIRENS IN THE DISTANCE SHRIVELED TIM'S intestines.

Damn. If those sirens were for them, they were screwed. A dozen thoughts rambled through his head. *Cops. Need a story. Identify myself. Identify Lucie?*

Crap. The Rizzo name, when it came to Chicago cops, always brought curiosity. And judgment.

As much as he hated to admit it, since dating Lucie, he'd

come to realize her paranoia about people looking down on her because of her last name wasn't paranoia.

Nope. Lucie paid the price for her father's misdeeds.

"Cops," the delivery guy said.

He made a move to bolt and Tim gripped his coat harder, holding him in place. "You're not going anywhere. If those sirens are for us, you got two choices. Either I turn you over to them or you agree to talk to me and I get rid of them."

"Turn me over? For what? All I did was deliver an envelope."

Pedestrians wandered both sides of the street, most of them sticking to the opposite side because of the torn-up sidewalk behind them. A young couple strode their way, eyeballing Tim still hanging on to Red Hat. Tim slid his badge from his back pocket and held it up for them.

The man nodded, steering the woman clear.

Tim glanced at Antoine, clearly steamed enough that his chef's whites were all he needed to stay warm. "You wanna tell him what was in that envelope? It might motivate him."

Antoine considered it for a few seconds then nodded. "Blackmail letter."

"What?"

The sirens grew closer and the sinking feeling in Tim's gut grew. If those cops were for them, he needed to get this moving, get the kid to cooperate. "Yep," Tim said. "And blackmail is a felony in Illinois. That'll get you anywhere from six to thirty years in prison. Oh, and the fine. You got twenty-five grand laying around for that?"

Even in the dark, the kid's face drained five shades lighter. He thought it over for three solid seconds.

"Hey. I'm just the messenger. You scared the crap out of me chasing me down. I'll tell you whatever."

Red lights bounced off the storefront window on the corner as a Chicago PD cruiser whipped into view.

"Uh-oh," Ro said. "Time to call the girls to action."

Lunatic Roseanne opened her coat and popped a button on her blouse. The messenger's head jerked back, his eyes zooming to Ro as she plumped her ample breasts. Tim sighed. How the hell did this stuff keep happening?

Lucie met his gaze, her eyes a little spooked. Who could blame her? What with a foot chase and her best friend flashing her rack?

"We're fine," Tim said. "Stay calm. Let me talk. That goes for everybody."

She nodded, but he didn't believe it. When it came to defending herself, his girl couldn't keep her mouth shut. Most of the time it was a twisted turn on. Pipsqueak Lucie Rizzo constantly ready for battle. Fearless. That was Lucie.

Throw Roseanne into it and the two of them were like Navy destroyers.

Only Tim couldn't balance that with his need to protect them, to make sure they stayed safe.

A crowd gathered and Tim lightened his grip on the delivery guy's jacket.

Two cops exited their vehicle, shoulders back in that command presence posture the academy pounded into cadets' heads.

As a former beat cop, that command presence had saved Tim's ass many a time.

The first cop, big guy, late thirties, pushed through the crowd. Tim glanced at his partner. Younger. Not as hard in the eyes. Rookie maybe.

"Break it up, everybody," the big guy said.

Obviously pinpointing Tim as the threat, he sized him up. Tim released the delivery guy, holding his hands up where the cops could see them. "Officers, I'm Detective Tim O'Brien. Chicago PD. My badge is in my inside jacket pocket."

"Let me see it. Slowly."

Keeping one hand in view, Tim reached into his pocket and retrieved his badge wallet, handing it over. Both cops checked his creds and handed them back.

"We got a call about an altercation. What's going on?"

"Domestic situation," Tim said.

Domestic? Total flyer.

He pointed to Lucie and the delivery guy. "They had an argument. He ran and she tackled him."

The cop jerked his chin at Antoine. "What about him?"

"They were in his office when the argument broke out. He was concerned and ran after them."

"How're you involved?"

Tim pointed at Lucie. "She's my girlfriend. I was meeting her. I walked up and saw her chasing this guy."

"What was the argument about?"

Good question. This freewheeling only took him so far.

"Stripper banger!"

This from Lucie, who, as he anticipated couldn't help herself.

Roseanne, who'd busted her ex-husband doing the nasty with strippers, gasped. "Evil." She stepped forward, breasts bouncing as she poked a finger. "Are you friends with that rat-bastard ex-husband of mine? I could see the two of you making the rounds at the clubs."

The older cop's eyes bugged out. It could have been Ro's cleavage on full display rather than the actual words, but he got a hold of himself and cleared his throat. "Someone tell me what's going on."

Lucie grabbed Ro's elbow and hauled her back a step

just in case she started swinging the luggage that doubled as a purse.

"He's dating my friend," Lucie said. "I heard from our other friend that he's going to strip clubs when he's supposed to be at work. He's dating one of the dancers."

"I am not," the delivery guy shrieked.

"Liar!"

And here we go. So much for Tim doing the talking. He pointed at Lucie. "You're killing me right now. You know that, right?"

"Damned stripper-bangers," Ro fumed. "We should castrate all you cheating man-whores."

The older cop pressed his thumb and middle finger into his eyes. "To think, this shift is only half over."

"I'm no stripper-banger," the delivery guy said. "I got a girl at home. I love her."

"Oh, *right.*"

"Roseanne," Tim said, "shut up."

Ro whipped to face him and he narrowed his eyes, the two of them in a brutal stare down that he'd win. No doubt. A solid ten seconds passed before she let out a huff. "Fine. But keep me away from that stripper-banger. You know how I am with that."

"Look," the older cop said, "does anyone want to press charges here?" He made eye contact with the delivery guy who, if Tim guessed right, might be considering it. If that happened, they'd be spilling the truth—all of it—because Tim wouldn't let Lucie go down on an assault charge. Not when the delivery guy had some explaining to do about that blackmail letter.

The guy shifted his gaze from Tim to Lucie and back to the cop. "I'm good."

"All right." The cop faced Lucie. "What about you?"

"No. Thank you, though."

He met Ro's gaze and grinned at her. "Something tells me you're the wildcard."

She held up a finger. "Where I come from, we don't let cops handle our issues. I'll deal with that stripper-banger myself."

"I'm sure you will." The cop waved a hand at Tim. "You got this under control?"

"We're good. Thanks."

The cops went back to their car, the younger one glancing back at Ro and smiling. If Joey were here, it'd be a war.

"Phew." Lucie pushed her palm into her forehead. "That was crazy."

"Yeah," he agreed. "Did you have to bust out the stripper banger line? It would have been easier to toss a stick of dynamite."

"It was the first thing I thought of. I thought you were stuck so I jumped in to help."

"She's right, O'Hottie. You were blowing it."

Control. *Stay in control.* Tim closed his eyes and forced out a long, slow stream of air.

"Hello?" Antoine said. "I'd like to know who sent this blackmail note. Plus, I'm freezing my ass off."

Still holding onto the delivery guy, Tim considered walking him back to Antoine's office.

If he did that, he'd run the risk of an accusation that he held him against his will.

Tim scanned the area. Coffee shop on the corner. A nice, open space with plenty of witnesses.

He shoved the delivery guy. "Let's go. We're buying you coffee."

5

LUCIE FOLLOWED TIM AND THE MESSENGER INTO THE COFFEE shop with Ro and Antoine in tow. Inside, only a few patrons sat at the half-dozen tables, but Tim beelined past them to a seating area in the back corner.

Rather than call attention to themselves—Ro's cleavage did enough of that—by not ordering, Lucie paused at the counter to grab a few drinks. That was her, a nice girl out for a chat with her friends.

The *sssshhhrrr* of the espresso machine sounded just as Ro stepped up and volunteered to help Lucie carry. By the time they got to the group, Tim was already deep into his questioning of their suspect. The pseudo stripper banger.

"What did we miss?"

"Not a lot," Tim said. "This is Ryan Bishop. He works for a private delivery service." He checked his notes. "Get There Fast messenger service."

Lucie shoved aside a couple of magazines and set three black coffees on the table. Ro added another two.

"Black. No sugar."

Tim, always ready to mainline caffeine, dove right in,

taking a long sip of the steaming coffee before continuing his interrogation. "You were paid to deliver that envelope?"

"Yeah. My boss called. He's a one-man operation. He does the daytime deliveries and some at night. If he can't do it, he pays me cash. But, you know, don't tell anyone because this is a good gig and I don't want to get him in trouble with the IRS."

"Or you," Antoine said. "Isn't that right?"

The guy, a kid really, probably no older than early twenties, shrugged one boney shoulder. "Well, sure. I got student loans to pay off."

"What time did he call you about this delivery?"

"Maybe 5:30. I had to pick up the envelope at his office and then deliver it. Traffic was nuts."

Tim jotted a note. "Where's his office?"

"Southwest side. He rents from his accountant. Cheaper than doing a lease on his own."

"That's handy at tax time," Ro said.

Lucie slashed her hand across her throat. "Shh."

"I'm just saying."

Tim shot them a look. "You two about done?"

They'd never be done and he knew it. Still, Lucie zipped her lips and found herself on the receiving end of a grunt from Antoine.

If he knew what was good for him, he'd keep his noises silent. Lucie didn't like being accused of stealing and when she proved her innocence, Antoine would owe her a giant— perhaps groveling—apology.

Now though, he sat forward, tapping one finger on the coffee table. "Did he inform you who wanted the envelope delivered?"

"Nah. He just tells me where to take it. I swear, I didn't know what was in it."

Puh-lease. He had to know. Lucie shook her head. "Why did you run then?"

"You started chasing me. It doesn't take a genius to figure out whatever was in that envelope pissed you off. I got scared."

Two girls—teenagers—entered the coffee shop, their giggles echoing in the quiet space. They bypassed the counter, obviously on their way to the ladies' room.

Tim held up the hand with his pen in it to silence the group. "All right. Pipe down." He pointed with the pen. "Ryan, get your boss on the phone."

The kid's lips peeled back. "Now?"

"No. Tomorrow. Yes, now. We need to know who sent this letter."

"Oh, come on, man. I only work for the guy. And he's not real nice. He's gonna be mad."

"Ask me if I care."

"Ask if *any* of us care," Lucie added.

On a sigh, Ryan dragged his phone out and scrolled. "I'm cooked after this."

"If you're telling the truth and we get what we need, I'll square it with him."

Ryan tapped the screen and handed the phone to Tim. "Hello? No. This isn't Ryan. My name is Tim O'Brien. I'm a detective with the Chicago police department."

And, oh wow. Tim never—ever—identified himself as a police officer unless on duty and now he'd done it twice in the last twenty minutes. Her man possessed a solid oak sense of honor. With that came his unwillingness to use his badge as leverage. Now, in an effort to help her, he'd obliterated his personal code of conduct.

"I'm calling," Tim said, "about the delivery Ryan just made to Antoine Durand... Yes, sir. That one. I'm not able to disclose the contents, but we need to locate the sender... No, sir. No name... Sir, it's imperative... Sorry, I'm not at liberty to say. Thank you, sir."

Tim hung up and handed the phone back. "A man called to schedule the delivery. The envelope was dropped off at the accountant's office and left with the receptionist. With cash payment. No information was exchanged."

Drat. The quick ride to Lucie being cleared had just hit a snag.

"I don't understand how people do business this way," Ro said. "Whatever happened to accountability?"

"Exactly why the sender used a private service. The larger delivery companies make you show identification."

Ryan's gaze bounced all over and then settled on Tim. "I did what you asked. Can I go?"

"Let me see your ID."

"Why?"

"So I know where to find you if I need you." He handed him his notepad. "Write your number down. And don't try giving me a fake one. I'll find you if I have to. And then I'll just be pissed that you wasted my time."

Ha! *Go, Tim.* How she loved a man who knew how to control a situation. So hot.

Two minutes later, Ryan hustled out of the coffee shop like a prisoner just sprung from death row.

"Well," Lucie said, "that got us nowhere."

Antoine stood and waved one hand. "I disagree. It's rather clear to me now."

Had he missed the whole conversation? The one that had garnered a big fat zilch? "What's clear?"

"You come to my office pretending to want to help and while you're there, I get a blackmail letter. Then we go through this whole charade and wind up with no information."

Just stop it. A familiar heat rose in her chest, tearing its way around her ribcage. "You can't believe I set this up."

"Sure I can. You're the only one who could have taken that recipe. What I'm stunned over is this elaborate plan you hatched so I would think you're trying to help." He let out a sarcastic snort. "That's brilliant."

"Hold on," Tim said.

Antoine whirled on him. "I will *not* hold on. I'm calling my lawyer."

Please. No lawyers.

Tim stood, got eye to eye with Antoine. "Why the lawyer? Call the police if you really think Lucie did it."

"The note said if I called the cops the recipe would be posted online. I can't have that. I've built a billion-dollar business on that recipe and I'm not risking it. "

He faced Lucie, his dark eyes direct and...mean. Something she'd never seen on the normally affable chef. "You really think I'd take your recipe? That I would do that?"

"All the evidence points that way." He waved his arms, gesturing around the coffee shop. "If you've gone to all this trouble already, I don't doubt you'll release it. My entire company is built on that recipe being a secret. If it wasn't you, someone else wrote that note. If I call the cops, they'll post the recipe. I'm sunk either way. I'm calling my lawyer and waiting for the next communication."

At 9:00 the following morning, Lucie strode from the Coco Barknell break room with a giant mug of coffee in hand. Yesterday had drained her to the point where her body had caved to exhaustion, but her mind refused to rest.

All night long, in her childhood room with the princess furniture, she'd dozed and jolted awake, dozed and jolted awake. All because her brain wouldn't shut down. *Find that recipe. Prove your innocence. Do something.* On and on it went, an endless loop of panic ravaging her already exhausted mind.

She sipped from her mug, thankful to coffee beans everywhere. "We have a lot to do today."

Ro looked up from her spot at the conference table where she too savored an oversized coffee. Her laptop sat open in front of her. "There's nothing online about the blackmail. It's staying quiet."

"Good."

Even with a blackmailer on the loose and Lucie being blamed, she had a business to run. One that included route and schedule adjustments to accommodate new dog-walking clients.

And recently abandoned ones, since Antoine had fired them.

"Luce," Ro said, "are you okay?"

Lucie set her mug down and sat across from Ro. "It's just another day in paradise, isn't it?"

"Amen, sister. I'm worried about you with this whole being fired thing. You care too much. Have we ever been fired before?"

Lucie's mind tripped back to last spring and the dognap-pings that had plagued her when the business barely supported her, never mind an entire staff. "Once. Remember Mr. Darcy?"

"Oh, that wack-job. Yes. He hired us back though."

"True, but he still fired us. That was the only time. I

intend to get Brie back as well. I can't have Antoine bad-mouthing us when we haven't done anything wrong."

Nothing sparked Lucie's wrath like being accused of a crime.

The whole of her adult life had been spent running from the mob princess moniker and some days, like today, the war felt endless. And futile.

Joey pushed through the office door bringing a blast of cold air with him. Her brother wore jeans, sneakers, and what looked like a sweatshirt under a light jacket. How he traipsed around a city known for its cold winters without a winter coat, she'd never understand. The man was a human furnace.

"Boo Thang," Felix squawked.

Something else she could have survived without, but he'd needed a home. Now she owned a mostly foul-mouthed parrot.

"Whoopsie," Ro said.

Joey halted. "What did he say?"

"Boo Thang," Felix said again.

Ro shook her fist at Lucie. "This damned bird. I know he got me out of prison, but does he have to repeat everything?"

"Boo Thang!"

"Why," Joey said, "is this pain in the ass calling me Boo Thang?"

Lucie wandered to the cage and slid the cover over it. It tended to settle their feisty bird. "Sorry, Felix. You need to learn though." She adjusted the cover, making sure the bottom was even all around before reclaiming her seat at the table. "Ro calls you Boo Thang when you're not around."

"Really?"

Ro tossed her hands in the air, her glare mutinous. "So what? You are my boo thang. Big deal."

"Hey, don't get crazy on me. I've been called worse."

At that, Lucie laughed.

Ro flicked her gaze to Joey, then blew him a kiss. Lucie nearly gagged.

But in a completely un-Joey move, he walked to Ro and kissed her on top of the head.

Aw, kinda sweet. In a disgusting way.

He continued to the organizer on the wall where Lucie kept the day's dog-walking schedule. "What happened with the chef last night? Did he find his stupid recipe?"

"No. The whole thing was a mess."

"Ransom note," Ro said.

"Who the hell kidnaps a recipe?"

Plenty of people. Lucie picked up her pen, circling it. "Someone looking to cash out quick. That recipe built a business worth billions. Part of the allure is the secrecy. Only Antoine and one executive know the entire recipe. Everyone else has bits of it. And there are only a few of those folks. If it gets released to the public, his business comes apart."

Her brother tucked the walking schedule in his back pocket and pursed his lips. "This note, what'd it say?"

"It said if Antoine called the cops, they'd post the recipe online and that he should wait for another communication."

A low whistle streamed from Joey's lips.

"He thinks I'm behind the whole thing. The Rizzo name isn't exactly synonymous with law-abiding citizenship."

"Here we go." Her idiot brother stroked his thumb and index finger together, creating a tiny violin. "Blah, blah, boo-fucking-hoo."

"Joey," Ro said, "knock it off. Antoine accused our Lucie of blackmail. And the rat-bastard fired us."

For whatever reason, the firing part grabbed his attention. Lucie being accused of blackmail? Not even a blip.

"Come on? The Ewok is gone?"

Lucie closed her eyes and said a quick Hail Mary. All these years, how had she not murdered him yet?

Each day, that accomplishment grew into a source of pride.

He waved them off. "I'll talk to Antoine."

Great. Now he wanted to play the muscle? "And what? Break his kneecaps? No. No talking."

The two of them stared at her, apparently stunned into silence that Lucie, the one always striving for truth and honor, would be satisfied waiting while someone thought poorly of her.

Ro cocked her head. "Are you sure you're okay?"

"I'm fine. Just because I don't want Joey making a stink doesn't mean I'm sitting around doing nothing. I'm making a plan."

Joey held up a finger. "*We're* making a plan. No one accuses Rizzos of stealing."

Well, no one but the federal government. But that was for a different day.

Ro smacked a hand on the table. "Exactly."

Her peeps. Joey, the Merchant of Wiseass and Ro, the drama queen. How awesome were they?

Twisted, but awesome. Maybe they all fought like crazy, but they stuck together. Always. Something Lucie had taken for granted in the past. She'd been too busy trying to rise above being a Rizzo. The shame of that settled in her stomach. Now? Every morning, she said a silent prayer of thanks. For everything. Particularly for a family, despite its reputation, that loved and protected her. "Thank you, guys. You're always there for me."

"Eh," Ro said, "that's what we do. Now, let's find the rat-bastard who stole this recipe."

Joey checked his watch. "I got half an hour before I have to leave to pick up Otis. You know how he gets when the schedule gets thrown."

Her brother. The mush.

Joey dropped into the seat next to Ro, eyed her for a few long seconds, and leaned toward her. "You look great."

What the heck had gotten into him today? Lucie pointed at him. "Who are you and what have you done with my brother?"

The joke fell flat while Joey and Ro made eyes at each other. Lucie contemplated giving them a few minutes alone. In her mind, Joey and Ro's relationship had three modes: Fighting, laughing, screwing.

The order of those things often changed, but the elements remained the same.

They put the P in passion. It worked for them, but Lucie? No way. She needed different. She needed what Detective Tim O'Brien provided. Rock solid and steady, they were a team with a similar sense of humor and values. Spending time with him instilled a sense of calm she'd never experienced. Joe Rizzo's daughter and a cop. Go figure? But Tim understood her, understood her drive to grow Coco Barknell into a Fortune 500 company. He was her partner in every way.

And he looked good naked.

What more could a girl want?

How about to not be caught in the middle of dustups requiring police involvement?

Lately, Tim's job didn't necessarily mix with the chaos

known as Lucie's life. She seemed to constantly be putting him in awkward positions. As horrible as she felt about that, she wasn't sure how to fix it.

And being accused of stealing a famous recipe wouldn't help.

"Okay," she said. "Let's get to work on a plan. I was up half the night, and I think we start by making a list of all the people who may have had access to Antoine's office."

She hopped out of her chair and walked to the rolling white board against the wall.

Blue marker in hand, she wrote SUSPECTS at the top of the board.

"Firefighters," Ro said.

"Employees," Joey added.

Lucie jotted both. "Police. They were on scene as the fire was being put out. One of them could have wandered upstairs."

Joey propped his hands on his head. "What about that back door Lucie came out of? The one that leads to the fire escape. Anyone could have climbed it."

"Ugh. He's right."

"Reporters," Ro said. "That fire was *all* over the news. And you know how aggressive reporters can be."

Lucie added REPORTERS to the list and stepped back. It was a start, but...

"What's wrong, Luce?"

Good old Ro. She knew Lucie's signals better than most.

"Something is bugging me. Why would someone want to do this to Antoine?"

"Easy," Joey said. "Greed."

Lucie tipped her head one way then the other, still studying the list. "Well, sure. I'm just wondering if there's more to it."

"Like what?"

"A vendetta. Maybe it's not about the money, but about ruining Antoine?"

"Revenge is a strong motivator," Ro said. "I'm crazy in love with your brother, but I'd neuter my stripper-banging ex-husband in a second."

Joey threw his arms up. "Here we go."

"No. She's right. Humiliation like that doesn't go away. I think we need to start investigating this list, but also find out if anyone had some sort of vendetta against Antoine."

"Honey," Ro said, "you don't get that rich and famous without crushing someone on your way to the top."

Lucie flicked the marker at Ro. "And when someone is that famous, their exploits are reported on. Widely. We can research it on the internet. See who hated Antoine enough to do something like this. We all know what a snake pit social media can be."

Joey checked his watch and stood. "I gotta go. But you know what we can also do?"

"What?"

"Hack into his emails."

That did it. Her brother was officially insane. "No. *That's* crazy. Way outside my comfort zone. What are you *thinking*?"

"You want people calling you a thief? A con woman? Is that in your comfort zone?"

"Joey," Ro said, "stop."

He gave her the classic Joey hard stare. As if that ever worked on Ro.

"You stay out of it." He turned back to Lucie. "You don't want people judging you." He waved his arms. "Ooh, I'm not a mob princess. Poor, poor me, my last name is Rizzo."

Lucie wanted to argue, wanted to rail on her brother, but...nothing. God help her, Joey was right.

"Luce, if you want answers quick? Then see what this guy has in his personal life. Think about the crap you email each day. Business problems, talking smack about people, all of it is in there."

"You want me to hack into someone's emails? Last I checked, that was illegal."

Joey grinned. "Only if we get caught."

Book of Life According to Dad. Absolute confirmation that their father's choices affected them in ways far more important than embarrassment. Those choices taught them—Joey particularly—that it was sometimes necessary to play outside the lines.

"Besides," Joey added, "what's the difference between hacking into someone's computer and rummaging through their files?"

Such a jerk. Totally had her on that one since she'd snooped in a former client's file cabinet to help prove he was running a scam.

"Damn you, Joey."

He held his hands wide. "It is what it is, Luce."

"Well, all of it is moot since none of us know how to hack."

"We don't need to." He gave her a smug grin. "I got a guy."

6

LUCIE AND RO STOOD ON THE SIDEWALK IN FRONT OF A THREE-story brick row home in West Town, a neighborhood on the near northwest side of Chicago.

For a guy who owed his bookie five grand, Joey's client seemed to live well. Considering the average home values in this neighborhood fell somewhere around $400,000.

Somehow, she'd expected different. Something seedier with overgrown weeds and broken light fixtures. Blacked out windows.

The windows might have been a stretch.

But, hey, maybe the guy was good at his job.

Leave it to Joey to come through. As much as she liked to nag him about giving up his bookie business, the fact that some degenerate gambler owed him $5,000 might have just helped her cause.

Should she do it, though? Resort to an illegal activity—one that might include jail time—to prove her innocence?

All this time, she'd held herself to higher standards than her father and brother. Lucie, the good one. The honest Rizzo.

How things changed.

Irony. Always a bitch.

She stood in the morning sunshine, the warm rays splashing over her cheeks, lifting her spirits a smidge. Ahead, nearly glowing stone steps led to a narrow porch and an oversized glass door that screamed contemporary. Whoever this hacker was, he had good taste.

"Am I really doing this?"

Ro glanced over at her. "Sister, you sure are."

"I mean, it's *illegal*. God help us if Joey didn't find all the bugs planted in our office because now the feds know what we're planning."

Heck, maybe this guy worked for the feds. Who knew?

After finding listening devices planted by federal agents spying on Dad, Joey did regular sweeps of the shop to ensure Lucie's privacy. The feds must have deemed Lucie a bore or assumed Joey, already known for his sweeps, would tear out any additional devices. Either way, Joey's weekly searches had since been a bust. Lucie tried not to be insulted by the idea of being irrelevant.

Ro pointed a finger. "Don't chicken out now. Someone is accusing you of stealing. This could ruin you. We're not using the information to commit fraud. It's *research*. The government does it all the time when they're building a case."

Point there. Dad spent two years in the clink and, although it had never come out in trial, the feds knew too much about Joe Rizzo's finances to not have employed a hacker or two.

Joey strode up, hands in his pockets, big shoulders back. "I walked Otis. Lauren is taking the next two walks so I have some time here."

"Thank you, Joey. We could have done this alone."

"My ass," he said. "This guy isn't dangerous, but he's shifty."

Excellent.

"He's agreed to help us?"

"Yeah. I called him. We're good."

"What did you promise him?"

"Don't worry about it."

Lucie latched on to the sleeve of her brother's jacket. "Please tell me you didn't let him off the hook for what he owes you."

"I said, don't worry about it."

He shrugged her off and headed to the front door. When Lucie shook her head, Ro slipped her arm over Lucie's shoulder. "Let it go. Whatever deal he made, it's his business."

"Yes, but $5,000 is a lot of money. Even if it's from a degenerate gambler."

"If you think he's worried about that, you don't know your brother at all."

"It's not the money. Well, it is the money, but... I don't know."

Her brother's legendary protectiveness should not include forgiving a debt. Not for her.

Joey rang the doorbell and waited. Nothing.

"Great," Ro said. "He knows we're coming, right?"

With that, Joey spun back and glared. Most people would melt from the force of that glare. Most people.

"Save it," Ro said. "You don't scare me, Joey Rizzo."

Joey whipped out his phone and shot off a text. He stood perfectly still, but the insane energy contained in his stiff shoulders sizzled in the cold air. He hopped off the porch and stared up at a second story window.

"Hey, dumbass! Get down here and open this door. Don't make me embarrass you."

Yeesh. The dumbass wasn't the only one embarrassed.

Ro let out one of her Queen-of-the-Universe sighs. "Do you have to yell like a savage?"

"Sometimes I do."

A middle-aged man appeared at the window and held his index finger up.

"If he bolts out the back door," Joey muttered. "I'll kill him."

"You know what?" Lucie held up her hands. "This isn't worth it. Forget it."

The front door swung open and the man waved them forward. "Did you have to yell? I have neighbors."

Joey took the stairs two at a time and faced off with his gambler buddy. "That was the point. You've been ducking me for three weeks."

"Sorry about that. I had—"

"I don't care. This is my sister, Lucie, and my girlfriend, Ro. Lucie needs help—and you're gonna give it to her."

The man's eyebrows hitched, and his gaze ping-ponged between Lucie and Joey. "Uh, sure. Sure. Come in." He held his hand to Lucie. "I'm Dean. Pleasure to meet you."

Nice manners. For a hacker. Which made Lucie even more curious. This guy, with his khaki pants and collared shirt, could be any one of the bankers she worked with before being downsized out of her finance job.

Inside, Joey pointed ahead of him to a set of stairs. At the end of the hallway was another door Lucie assumed accessed a first-floor unit.

Condos.

"You can go up," Dean said. "Second floor is mine."

Lucie and Ro climbed the stairs while Joey and Dean

stood on the landing, whispering something about a bad bet and making good.

By the time Lucie and Ro reached the second floor, Joey and Dean clomped up behind them.

"We're all set," Joey said.

"You're sure?"

"Yep." He smacked Dean on the back. "Whatever you need. Let's get started. I got dogs to walk."

"So," Lucie said, "how exactly are we doing this?"

Dean sat at his desk, surrounded by Lucie, Joey, and Ro. For a hacker, his setup was rather mundane. An oversized monitor, an ergonomic keyboard—probably a must in his line of work—and a laptop.

No fancy command center for this guy. Did it matter? Probably not, but she'd been questioning everything about this adventure since they'd left Coco Barknell, so why not his choice of equipment?

If Tim found out about this, he'd have a fit.

Everything else? The illegal hacking, the dishonesty, the invasion of Antoine's privacy, she could live with. Her justification came in the form of proving her innocence. Her only intent here was to clear her name and find the real thief. Not use Antoine's personal information for nefarious purposes.

Dean pulled up an email account. "We'll try a worm."

"A worm?"

"Yes. An email that contains a virus. I'm including a key logger that'll log any keystrokes. If he types a password, the key logger captures it and sends it to my server."

Holy cow, Lucie would never again feel comfortable logging into her bank account. "And you won't get caught?"

Dean looked up with a *you're-kidding-me-right?* stare. Apparently, Lucie had insulted his highness. Who'd have thought hackers were so sensitive?

"Sorry," she said, "this criminal stuff is new to me. Can I ask what your credentials are?"

Dean snorted, but when Lucie continued to eyeball him, he straightened up. "You're serious?"

"Welcome to my world, dude," Joey said.

Avoiding her scrutiny, Dean went back to his keyboard, engulfing himself in what must have been his own personal security blanket. "My credentials. Huh. Well, let's see, I hacked into a major bank recently. That was legit. Corporate hired me as part of a security review. They wanted to see if I could get through their firewall."

Online banking? Never again. "How did that go?"

"For me? Great. For them. Not so good."

Joey tapped his watch. "Tick-tock, Luce. Time is money."

If this guy was good enough to be hired by a major bank, he knew his stuff. "Okay. But I don't want to look."

Now Dean flat out laughed. "Pardon?"

"You look. Just scroll through his account and tell me if anything is suspicious."

Yes, that would work. If she didn't actually *see* the emails, she wouldn't have to feel guilty.

"That's a new one. You realize it's still illegal, right? No matter how you slice it, it's unauthorized access."

Having heard enough, Joey gave Dean a backhanded slap on the shoulder. "Let her justify it however she likes. She's weird that way."

"Fine. I'll need his email address."

On her phone, Lucie pulled up her contact list, found Antoine's name, and passed the phone to Dean.

The hacker went to work, crafting an email from the local power company. Fake or not, the correspondence looked horrifyingly official. Logo and everything.

"Wow," she said, "seriously scary."

"Eh. This is nothing."

He hit send and sat back. "Now we wait and see if he opens it. How quick is he with his email?"

They'd have to sit here and wait? That might take hours. Lucie grunted. "Normally he gets back to me in a few hours."

"But," Ro said, "his business is closed right now. Maybe he'll be quicker."

Lucie sure hoped so.

Ro nudged closer. "Hey, can we do this to my rat-bastard ex? He's behind on his support payments. If he's spending my money on strippers, I'll crucify him."

Unbelievable. Ro's ex might be a schmuck, but he deserved his privacy. "No, we're *not* doing that. While we're waiting, I'll run down some of the other leads we discussed this morning. Dean, can you call me with this information?"

The hacker shrugged. "Sure. But if he's smart, he won't open it. Just so you know. This whole thing could be a bust."

AFTER DETERMINING THE CLOSEST FIREHOUSE TO RESTAURANT Durand, Lucie and Ro swung by the Bernards' to pick up Josie and Fannie, aka the Ninja Bitches. The girls were always on point when it came to covert missions. Part of their allure was how darned cute they were. All people saw were a couple of Shih-Tzus decked out in bejeweled Coco Barknell coats and collars. What they didn't see was the underlying survival instinct these girls possessed.

If prompted, they'd take a leg off. Gnaw right through the bone.

Thus, the Ninja Bitch moniker.

Which made them perfect for investigative uses. Cute, tough, smart. An all-around killer combo.

Lucie found street parking, and they hoofed it the two city blocks to the firehouse. Beside her, Ro, in her typical sky-high heels, *click-click-clicked* down the sidewalk as Fannie kept her nose to the ground.

A high-heeled dog walker. Who'd believe that? Exactly no one. "You should have worn flat shoes."

"Why?"

"You think these firemen will believe we're canvassing the neighborhood and passing out brochures with you in six-inch heels?"

Fannie stopped to water a towering oak tree. Ro held one finger up. "First of all, they're only five inches. These *are* my walking shoes. I could go five miles in these. Second of all, I'll pop a button on my blouse and, believe me, those boys won't be looking at my shoes."

She opened her coat and one-handed—yes, she'd become an expert by now—released the extra button on her blouse that would give the world an insanely obvious view of her cleavage. Porn stars showed less skin.

Ro adjusted the opening of her blouse, made a *hmmm* noise, then threw herself forward, bending at the waist.

Josie and Fannie flinched, leaping sideways with a growl.

Lucie cracked up. "Easy, girls. Just ignore the crazy lady."

"Listen, a push-up bra only goes so far."

Ro flipped her head back up, then gave her boobs a plump. Right in the middle of the sidewalk.

Alrighty. Lucie scanned the windows of the surrounding homes hoping they didn't have an audience. So much for a covert operation.

"Okay," Ro said, still scrutinizing her breasts. "Now we're

talking. As soon as those boys see the boobage, they'll be putty in your hands."

Who needed waterboarding when Ro's chest was available? "Maybe we should lease your rack to the CIA."

"Hardy-har. You won't be cracking wise in a few minutes."

"Let me do the talking," Lucie said. "I have the brochures."

Nothing like multitasking. The plan was simple. They'd march inside, distribute Coco Barknell brochures to the firefighters, and hopefully collect some names.

Talk about a half-baked scheme. Chances of this leading somewhere were nil, but Lucie never let that stop her.

They swung through the entrance with the Bitches leading the way. A plump, middle-aged receptionist locked eyes on the dogs in their rhinestone leather bomber jackets and an immediate smile split her face.

As mom would say, in like Flynn.

"Hello, ladies," the woman said, "how can I help you?"

Lucie slid a business card and a brochure from the outside pocket of her messenger bag. "Hi. I'm Lucie from Coco Barknell. This is my partner, Roseanne. We're walking the neighborhood handing out brochures and wondered if we could give some to the staff."

A firefighter the size of a 747 appeared in the doorway separating reception from the guts of the firehouse.

Lucie smiled a greeting and he nodded, but his attention shifted...elsewhere.

Elsewhere being the 36Ds to Lucie's right.

The receptionist shook her head as Ro gave Lucie the *I-told-you-so* look. Hips swinging, Ro sauntered to the firefighter. "Hello." She held out her hand. "I'm Roseanne from Coco Barknell. We're a dog-walking/pet accessory company.

This is Fannie. She's wearing one of our latest designs. Fabulous, no?"

"Uh."

"Exactly!" Ro swung back to Lucie. "See? He's speechless."

He was speechless all right.

Ro flapped some brochures against the firefighter's chest. "We were hoping to give you boys these flyers."

"Uh."

"Excellent." Ro shoved by the guy, with Fannie trotting along.

Later, Lucie would be horrified. Right now? Not so much.

Lucie peered down at the receptionist's pinched mouth. Ro had just steamrolled this poor woman. Rather, Ro's boobs had steamrolled her.

"I'm sorry," Lucie said. "As you can see, she's passionate about our company."

"Oh, I see." The woman waved her hand. "Go on back. I think they're all eating. First door on your left."

"Thank you."

Once inside, Lucie walked down the long corridor. In full investigative mode, she paused in front of a bulletin board to snoop.

Ro's voice carried from what Lucie assumed was a kitchen or common area. "We also custom design accessories," she was saying. "Tell your wives and girlfriends. There are photos in the brochures. Our most popular collar is the pink one with rhinestones."

"These are handmade?" one of the men asked.

"Yes. Every one of them. I design them and our team of seamstresses does all the sewing. We're so confident, we offer a money back guarantee."

While Ro did her magic, Lucie perused the bulletin board. Local charity events, community plays, restaurant menus, the usual. She skimmed a memo informing employees that, due to a transparency policy, all city of Chicago employees' departments, positions, and salaries would be listed on the city's website.

Now that might be something to follow-up on.

She'd have to hunt down that list. It probably wouldn't give her specifics—she'd never get that lucky—as to which house the firefighters were assigned to, but it might be a start with names.

Another document peeked out from under one of the menus. Lucie lifted the menu away to find a white sheet of paper announcing a baby pool for one of the firefighters. Thank God for men. They'd bet on just about anything. Her brother the bookie counted on it.

She glanced left then right. No one. Quickly, she slid her phone from her jacket pocket and snapped photos of all the names, phone numbers, and email addresses on the list.

Lucie stowed her camera and poked her head into the kitchen/common area. Seven men sat around a large farm table. One of them held Fannie's leash while Ro moved around the table, slapping brochures in front of the men. And if she bent forward a wee bit too much, none of the men seemed to mind. One guy may have had spittle running down his chin.

"There are coupons in here," Ro said. "Twenty percent off a purchase. That's good for dog walking, too, so take advantage of it." She winked at spittle guy. "I promise you won't be disappointed."

Lawdy.

Ro nodded and continued handing out brochures. "Here

are my business cards. If you'd like to be added to our mailing list, write your name and email on the back."

Brilliant. Rather than break Ro's momentum, Lucie headed back to the lobby to pump the receptionist for information. Divide and conquer.

Lucie led Josie down the hall, her little nails' *tippety-tapping* alerting the receptionist of their arrival.

Using her free hand, Lucie dug in the outside pocket of her messenger bag for more brochures. "I thought I'd leave some extras with you. Maybe for the employees who aren't here? Would that be okay?"

The receptionist pursed her lips as if Lucie wanted to hand her anthrax. People were so paranoid these days.

The receptionist held her hand out. "Sure. I'll make sure the other shifts get them. If you want all the shifts and admins to have them, I'd need about thirty."

Thirty. Based on the number of names Lucie found on the baby pool list, that meant most of the employees had signed up.

If she found the employee list on the city's website, she could cross check the names from the baby pool to see which folks were firefighters and which were admins.

Dang it. If only she could get a breakdown of who was on which shift.

She counted out the requisite number of brochures and, taking Ro's lead, handed over a stack of her business cards. "If anyone has any questions, they can call me."

The receptionist tapped the photo on the cover of the brochure. "Are these the same two dogs?"

Observant woman. Then again, who could resist all that cuteness? "Yes. The one on the left is Josie." Lucie glanced down. "That's this pretty girl. Fannie is her sister. We test a lot of our products on them. That pink collar is our bestseller."

In the last six months they'd given away dozens of those collars to newsletter subscribers.

Freebies.

Who didn't love free? "In fact, you all have been so nice, why don't I do a drawing for all your employees? I wouldn't want to leave the later shifts out. Maybe a custom coat and collar?"

The receptionist's eyes lit up. "Really? You'd do that?"

"Sure. You're civil servants. It's the least we could do. All I'd need is everyone's names."

"Oh." She glanced down, tapping her fingers against the desk. "I'm not sure if I can give you that. I mean, they're all on the website, but that doesn't list specific firehouses."

Shoot.

"Hmmm, that would be such a shame. I've run into this before, though, and completely understand. The last time it happened, the manager gave me first names and shifts only. The manager then passed my card on to the winner. That way I didn't have any personal info."

The receptionist twisted her mouth one way then the other, clearly pondering Lucie's wisdom. "The names *are* on the website. And I wouldn't be giving any personal information out." She smacked her hand on the desk. "Let's do it. The gang here loves when people do things for them."

Jackpot.

Josie barked once, followed by two more rapid yips. Pee signal. "Whoopsie. She has to piddle. How about I take her out and come back for the list?"

The receptionist spun to her computer. "I have the names in a spreadsheet. I'll have it ready when you get back."

"Perfect." Between what Ro collected from the firefighters, the names on the bulletin board, the transparency list, and what the receptionist gave them, they should be able to narrow down which firefighters had been at the restaurant yesterday.

By six o'clock, Lucie had dealt with some minor customer scheduling issues, processed payroll, and moved on to creating a spreadsheet containing the firefighters' names.

Ro sat at her own desk, answering emails and waiting for Joey to pick her up for—whatever it was they did on their downtime. Lucie didn't want to know.

Blech.

Back to the spreadsheet.

"Now," she said to Ro, "all I have to do is match the first names from the receptionist's list to what you got from the men and the baby pool list, then crosscheck it with the transparency file from the city's website. Easy."

Ro stared at her with eyes that flashed a red vacancy sign. *Blink, blink. Blink, blink.* "You lost me, but as long as you know what you're doing, I don't care."

Lucie's phone rang. She glanced down to see *O'Hottie* lighting up the screen. He complained about the nickname, but down deep, he had to like it. Lucie sure did.

"Hiya, handsome."

"My girl. What are you doing?"

Tricky business here. Tim didn't like her involved in what he termed screwball investigations. Sympathetic to the plight of her cop boyfriend, she chose not to put him in awkward positions by filling him in on every detail.

Right now, this firefighter thing hadn't quite materialized into anything and, in Lucie's mind, wasn't worth irritating her beloved.

Yes, she'd protect him from this.

What a crock. Protect herself from a lecture was more like it.

She flicked a gaze at her laptop screen. "I'm working on a spreadsheet."

So she'd left out a few minor details.

"Gee, that sounds fun. Can I drag you away?"

"What'd you have in mind, sailor?"

Across the room, Ro rolled her eyes. Lucie stuck her tongue out. According to Ro, Lucie stunk at seduction. Maybe she did, but Tim never seemed to mind.

"I'm on my way home," he said. "I can pick up dinner from the Italian place you like and we'll watch a movie."

And *other* things, Lucie presumed.

Stolen recipe or not, she wanted time with her man. Again, she glanced at the spreadsheet. *Wait on it.* Tonight, after she got home from Tim's, she'd tackle it. "I'd love that."

"See you at my place. Be ready for a long night."

Men.

Lucie disconnected, saved the file, and stowed her laptop in her messenger bag. Along with the manila folder containing all the paperwork and notes from the trip to the fire station.

"I'm leaving," she said to Ro, who furiously banged on her keyboard. "I'll finish this spreadsheet later. I've got a hot Irishman to do."

Forty-five minutes later, Lucie walked through Tim's front door using—*eh-hem*—the key he'd given her.

Her hot Irishman stood at the dining table in his favorite track pants with the rip at the knee and a T-shirt tight enough to send Lucie's mind straight to the gutter.

"Got all your favorites," he said, piling a plate high with pasta. "Major calories tonight, babe."

Such a sweet guy. "I do adore you, Tim O'Brien."

He hit her with one of his flashing O'Hottie smiles and a hard yearning sparked in Lucie's core. Tim made her... happy. Sure, they argued and occasionally disagreed, but her life with him, despite the craziness of the last few months, brought peace and calm.

Limited drama.

She set her messenger bag on the sofa and walked to the table, where she smacked a kiss on him. Full frontal, all tongue.

Naughty Lucie.

"Mmmm." he said, "I think it's gonna be a good night."

"I don't think. I know."

Lucie moved the loaded plates to their respective spots while Tim poured wine. Her man was more of a beer guy, but with Italian food he went for red wine. One of the many things she'd learned over these last six months with him.

After settling in, Lucie inhaled the fresh garlic and cheese. Her stomach let out a rumble.

"Did you skip lunch again?"

She thought back. "I forgot."

"Luce, come on. With how hard you run yourself, your body needs fuel. At least a protein bar."

"I know. But I was...busy." *Snooping around a firehouse.*

"What was so important that you couldn't eat?"

She broke off a hunk of bread. "I don't know. Stuff. I'm running a business. There's not enough time for it all."

Not going there. No, sir. If he knew she and Ro took on Mission Firefighter...yikes. She didn't even want to ponder it. Putting that out into the universe would only start an argument.

Refusing to look at him, she shoved a forkful of broccoli and cavatelli into her mouth and waited for the explosion of flavor. "Wow, this is really good tonight."

Tim set his fork down, sat back, and narrowed his eyes. The focused detective stare. "You're lying."

Oh, boy. Time for the Lucie soft shoe.

"I'm not. The food *is* good."

"Ha. You know that's not what I'm talking about. Tell me what you did today."

Fat chance. She pretended to study her plate. "Now that I think about it, they may have put a bit too much garlic in here."

Head still dipped, she stole another peek as he pushed his plate to the side and rested his elbows on the table.

I'm cooked.

"You were investigating again, weren't you? And don't lie. I know you."

Okay. She wouldn't lie. She'd just sit here. Quietly. Not saying a word.

"Crap," he said, his voice rising to that extra-special I'm-getting-pissed level. "Tell me everything."

Telling him everything included admitting making a deal with a hacker. And *that* couldn't happen.

Firehouse. Definitely the way to go.

Playing it cool, Lucie continued eating. "Truly, it wasn't a big deal. I made a list of possible suspects, which, by the way, I'm happy to share with you."

"Gee. Thanks."

"You're quite welcome."

Under the table, Tim's bare foot smacked against the floor like a jackhammer. The angry foot, Lucie called it.

"How did you develop this list?"

She set her fork down and slid her plate away. "Simple. I thought of all the people who had access to Antoine's office during the fire. Employees, first responders, etc."

Tim closed his eyes and whispered something Lucie couldn't quite make out.

"Being the brilliant business women we are, Ro and I paid a visit to the firehouse near the restaurant."

Tim opened his eyes. "A visit?"

"We brought a bunch of brochures and told the guys we were canvassing the area. Trust me, they bought our cover story. Really, it was a double win because a lot of them signed up for our newsletter. I'm sure Ro's half unbuttoned blouse didn't hurt."

"Good God."

"I know. But I have to say, in a room full of alpha males, a little—well, a lot—of cleavage, goes a long way. She's an ace. Makes it look sexy. Me? I'd look like an idiot."

"You're babbling."

What did he expect when he interrogated her like some common thug. "You're making me nervous with that detective stare." She flapped her arms. "We went to a firehouse, big deal."

"There's nothing else?"

For this, she'd have to look at him. Straight on.

And lie.

Which would shred her intestines like nothing before. This man trusted her. Betraying that trust meant keeping Joey and the hacker out of it.

Darn it. She should have never gone along with the hacking. That *had* to be a federal crime. Had to be.

"There's more, but it's not major. We went to the firehouse, then I talked the receptionist into giving me a staff list."

"She *gave* it to you?"

"Not exactly."

The next five minutes were spent in a lightning round of questions and answers.

"I think I have a complete list of all the employees at the firehouse. All that's left is to crosscheck it with the online database for city employees."

He nodded. "The transparency list. I know it well. I'm on it."

"I'm hoping the list will tell me if the employee is a firefighter or an admin. Plus, the list the receptionist gave me has all the shifts. I can narrow down which firefighters might have been at the restaurant based on the shift they worked."

"All right, Columbo," Tim said. "Show me this spreadsheet."

Whoa. Hold on one second. Tim had major issues with her playing detective. Therefore, he either wanted to dissuade her from further investigating by eliminating her theories, or...he wanted to help.

Nah. Couldn't be.

Could it?

Tim helping didn't happen a lot. Mostly because she chose not to involve him in Rizzo madness. He'd worked too hard for his career to have it compromised.

Lucie bit her bottom lip. "You want to see my spreadsheet? Why?"

He laughed. "Because I know you. I can talk until I pass

out, but you'll continue investigating. As crazy as it makes me, I love that about you. Your drive to make things right. I'm gonna help you. Hopefully it won't take all night and I'll still get laid."

Her man. She hopped up and ran around the table, throwing her arms around him and kissing him hard on the mouth. God, she loved him. She pulled back, set her hands on his cheeks, tracing the light freckles with her thumbs. "Thank you."

He smiled and his green eyes twinkled under the glow of the hanging light fixture. "You're welcome. Get your laptop while I finish my dinner."

———

"Okay," Tim said. "What you have here is three shifts. Red, blue, green. We need to know which shift worked yesterday. Do you have that?"

"No. The receptionist's info didn't include that."

He stood behind her, reading the data displayed on her laptop, occasionally leaning forward to point to something on screen. The closeness, that brief, solid contact, brought a sense of...what?

Lust.

Happiness.

Security.

The down deep confidence that, despite his job, he'd help her through this. Together, they'd figure it out.

"Download that transparency list. We can separate the fire department staff and then sort alphabetically to match it with what you have. While you're doing that, there's an online shift calendar for the fire department. I'll check that."

Two minutes later, Lucie had the list downloaded

—*thank you, City of Chicago*—and merged it with her data. After resorting and eliminating duplicates, thirty names remained.

"Bam," Lucie said. "These are all the firefighters and paramedics that work in that firehouse."

"According to this link, red shift worked yesterday."

Back to her spreadsheet Lucie went, sorting it by shift and...*voila*. All red shift members.

"Email me that list of names. I'll print it out."

She swiveled sideways and grabbed his wrist. She couldn't have him digging too hard on this. Not with the risks it posed to his career. "Please don't get in trouble."

"I won't. Firefighters are subject to background investigations, but that doesn't mean they're all saints. We'll search online and see if we can find anything on them."

He bent low and kissed her softly, lingering for a few seconds. Lucie's pulse kicked up. How long exactly had it been since they'd had sex? Made luuuvvvv...

Not that long. But when he kissed her like that? Could've been a lifetime.

Before things got too crazy and she had the opportunity to body slam him on the table, Tim backed away.

"Later," he said.

"I will count on that, mister."

He flashed her the wicked *I-will-make-you-howl* smile then wandered off leaving her to fantasize alone. She contemplated following him, but really, they were both distracted. And she wanted to be able to focus on the big guy. The big, hot, *naked* guy with the muscles and adorable freckles and...oooh-eee. *Naughty, Lucie.*

She swung back to her laptop and emailed Tim the spreadsheet, adding a one-liner about the things she'd do to him when she got him to a bed. Who said she sucked at seduction?

Just as she hit send, he walked across the hall to the spare bedroom/office, his laptop in hand.

"I just sent the email."

"I see that," he said. "Careful what you wish for, Luce."

Heh, heh, heh.

Lucie's phone rang, disrupting her X-rated thoughts about hot Irish detectives.

She glanced at the screen. Dean. Hacker extraordinaire.

All day he'd been silent. Now he calls?

She scooped up the phone, glancing at the empty foyer and the doorway to where Tim was busy printing that spreadsheet. If she could make this quick...

She tapped the screen before the call went to voicemail. "This is Lucie."

"Hi, it's Dean. Uh, from this morning?"

She checked the hallway again. No sign of Tim. "Hi, Dean."

"Your guy opened the email."

Yes! "He did?" Lucie fought the urge to hop out of her chair and do a butt wiggle. Which might be hard to explain to Tim. Since he'd just stepped into the hallway carrying a couple sheets of paper.

Darn it.

"Wow," she said, watching as Tim set his laptop in the spot beside her. "That's...uh...great. Did you find anything?"

Tim eyed her, his mouth twisting as he listened to her end of the conversation.

"He gets a ton of correspondence. And, man, he doesn't pull any punches."

"*Really.*"

"If you want to swing by here, I can go through the emails with you. There's one you'll want to see."

Tim's gaze was on her. Call it the burn of curiosity that came with dating a detective. Suddenly she had to pee. She smiled at him, offering a thumbs-up. Thumbs-up? What for? Now she'd have to explain. Blame it on the flop-peeing distracting her.

Whatever. She shook it off as her scrambled brain attempted a coherent thought. *Dean. An email she'll want to see.* "That sounds good. What does the email say?"

"It's a ransom note."

7

"A RANSOM NOTE?" LUCIE BLURTED, IMMEDIATELY SMACKING herself on the head.

There went the whole keeping-the-hacker-from-Tim theory.

O'Hottie spun on his chair, now fully facing her, his eyes narrowed. "What ransom note?"

"Um, Dean? Can I call you back?"

"Sure. I wouldn't take too long though. The note says they'll make contact at 9:00 tonight."

Lucie checked the clock on her laptop. Less than ninety minutes.

Her tummy did a massive flip. Why did she feel like the girl about to get smacked with a ruler by Sister Ophelia?

She stared at her laptop screen, willing some explanation to magically appear, but...nothing.

"Luce, what's going on?"

She could lie. Tell him it was something about the first note delivered to Antoine. Play it off like nothing. But he knew her. He'd see through that open window of a lie.

Fess up.

That's what she'd do. Just put it out there, hope he understood her need to break any number of federal laws by utilizing a hacker.

One who owed her bookie brother $5,000.

Oy, that sounded bad.

Slowly, she slid sideways and faced him. Looking into those pretty green eyes, she reconsidered the value of the truth. If she lost him over this, she'd be devastated.

Was it worth the risk?

No lying.

He deserved better.

Like she'd done so many times as the daughter of a mob boss, she pushed her shoulders back and lifted her chin. Ready to face the battle.

"You won't like it," she said.

"I gathered that."

She latched onto his forearms and squeezed. "But, please, hear me out."

He let out a long, quiet sigh. "Ah, Luce. What'd you do?"

"You know me. You *know* I need a plan for everything."

"Yeah. I'm *aware*."

She put up her hand. "Before you lecture me about screwball investigations, you wouldn't sit around and let something like this ruin your reputation, would you?"

She had him there. Some of the stiffness left his shoulders. She let out a small breath. So far, so good. At least he wasn't showing her the door.

"All right," he said. "Tell me."

"Just, please, stay calm."

Tim closed his eyes. His lips moved, spilling out something Lucie couldn't hear. He did that—a lot—when she frustrated him.

"Okay." She squeezed his arms again. "Joey knows someone who is..."

He opened his eyes. "What?"

Oh, hell. She might as well just spit it out. Before this was over, she'd have to admit it anyway. "A hacker. He owed Joey $5,000 from a bet that went bad."

Tim shot out of the chair and stalked the hallway leading to his bedroom. When he reached the end, he swiveled back, circling one hand in the air as if he wanted to say something, to really go off, but...nothing.

Which was probably worse.

Her lifetime included dealing with men who yelled. *That* she knew what to do with. Silence? Horrible.

She pushed out of her chair, but stayed in her spot. "It's not as bad as it sounds. It's a... friendly...relationship."

Coercion aside.

Tim completed another lap and stopped in the middle of the hallway, his hands propped on his hips. "Don't even start justifying. This is bullshit. You know it. A hacker! Are you nuts? Wait. No. Forget that. I know the answer. Why I'm shocked you lunatics would do this astounds me. *Astounds* me!"

"It's not—" He glared at her hard enough to stop her cold. Frustration mounted and she flapped her arms. Damned man twisting her all up. "I'm telling you the truth. I don't want you thinking Joey threatened to break his legs. Or whatever."

"That makes me feel a *lot* better."

"I know what it sounds like."

"Honey, you can't know. If you did you wouldn't have done it. Damn it, Luce. We're talking federal penalties here. What the hell are you looking for?"

She scrunched her nose and rolled her hand as if it

might help the words flow. "We're...uh...hacking Antoine's email to see if he's having a problem with anyone. You know, enemies."

"Enemies. Perfect."

"We're just looking for leads. We wouldn't have done anything else with his emails."

His gaze steady on hers, Tim shook his head. The stiffness in his shoulders, his rigid control, told her all she needed to know about the emotion spewing inside him. "I should walk away. Even for you, this is pushing it."

"I know you're mad. You have every reason to be."

His eyes bulged and his cheeks turned a weird shade of reddish purple that forced Lucie back a step. "Mad? I'm beyond that. You've compromised yourself, your brother, and me. Now I'm an accomplice."

Ew. She hadn't considered that. By telling the truth, she'd just opened him up to charges.

"I—"

"No. Don't say anything." He put his hands out, then pounded his fists on his head. "You're killing me. The blood pressure alone should give me a seizure. Damn it!"

He spun away from her, storming the hallway again. Once, twice, three times. Finally, he stopped, drew a long pull of air through his nose.

"I'm sorry," she said. "I shouldn't have told you."

"You shouldn't have done it." He held his hands out again. "Too late. Forget it. Let's deal with it. Tell me what this guy did?"

Reasonable Tim. And he'd yet to boot her out.

Good. She stiff-spined it, shoring herself up. "He sent a virus to Antoine's email. If Antoine opened the email, Dean —that's the hacker—would have access to his account."

"Do you have any idea how many laws you've broken?"

"A lot?"

He peered down at the floor, puffed up his cheeks and blew out a long breath. "What did he say about a ransom note? A second one?"

Lucie shrugged. "I assume. It says they'll make contact again at 9:00. He told me I could come over and he'd go through the emails with me."

"Tonight?"

"Yes. But I was here, so I got nervous and told him I'd call him back. I knew you'd be upset."

Now his mouth dropped open, his head dipping from the weight of it. "You would go to some dude's house—someone you don't even know—by yourself? Without telling me?"

Yes.

She winced.

No.

Eh. Maybe? "I don't know. And that's the truth. I didn't have a chance to think about it."

"First of all," he said, "the answer is no, you would *not* do that. I don't care what kind of shitstorm you're in, you tell me about it. Am I mad? Bet your cute little ass I am. It puts me in an impossible position. A detective helping his girlfriend break laws doesn't have a chance at career longevity."

"Which is why I didn't want to tell you."

"Second of all, you going there alone isn't an option. Ever. Got that?" He shook his head again, lifted his hands. "*Damn it.* You just can't stay out of trouble."

He stomped into his bedroom, returned a second later with sneakers in hand, and dropped into the chair at the end of the table. After ripping at his laces, he jammed the shoes on his feet, retying them with harsh tugs.

"I can't believe I'm about to say this, but I'm going with

you. We're gonna see what this guy has. And then I'll figure out what to do."

"You can't go with me. I don't want you at risk. I'll call Joey. He'll go."

"Well, babe, too late now. I know a crime has been committed. I'm already in it. Might as well see it through."

"Tim, I'm so sorry."

He set his feet on the floor and met her gaze. The playfulness from earlier, all that sparkly lust, had disappeared, leaving a dead stare. "Are you?"

That set her back some. "Of course I am."

"Then why do you keep doing this crap? Every time. I ask you to stay out of it and yet, you run one of your batshit investigations. I *get* you're at war with being Joe Rizzo's kid. I don't understand how it feels, but I know it drives you. What scares the hell out of me is what it'll take to get you to stop."

"I don't know."

"Well, you need to figure it out. I can't keep doing this. Now let's go see what this guy has. We're on the clock."

DEAN OPENED HIS FRONT DOOR, TOOK ONE LOOK AT THE stranger with Lucie, and his eyes got all shifty.

It wasn't a look preppy Dean wore well.

"Relax." Lucie held up her gloved hands. "This is Tim. My boyfriend."

She'd leave out the part about him being a cop.

"You didn't tell me you were bringing anyone."

"Well," Tim said, "deal with it. She's not going to a stranger's place—at night—by herself."

Peeing match. Time to rein these boys in. She pushed

around Dean, inviting herself inside. "It's fine. Tim is up to speed on everything."

With Lucie already inside, Dean stepped back, allowing Tim access. They followed Dean to the living room. His laptop sat open on a slick, glass-topped coffee table next to a mug of what smelled like fresh ground coffee.

He slid onto the couch. "Take a look at this. I've been watching his emails."

Lucie and Tim remained standing, but stared down at the screen. "This is the ransom note?"

"Yeah. Right here."

He clicked on the email, let it load, and handed the laptop to Lucie.

Do not call the police (or any law enforcement). We have your recipe (proof attached) and will post it online if you do not pay us two million dollars.

You have until 11:00 AM Friday to get the money. Only small, unmarked bills. The money drop will be at Cliffside Park. Go in at the east entrance and follow the path to the sixth bench. There is a hollowed-out tree behind the bench. Put the money in there. We WILL be watching. No funny stuff.

If you cooperate, we will not release the recipe. Try anything and the recipe will be released.

Behind her, Tim made a humming noise. "They're giving him time to pull the money together."

Not everyone had two mil in cash lying around. "Whoever this person is understands it could take a day for him to shift things around."

"Anyone with an investment account knows that. It doesn't narrow the field."

Tim waved at the laptop. "Anything else we should see?"

Dean shrugged. "Normal stuff. Disgruntled employee. A

vendor who hasn't gotten paid and, oh yeah, a friend of his is pissed about some invitation he didn't get to a dinner."

Pissed off friend? Lucie cocked her head. "What dinner?"

"Antoine's birthday. The pissed guy appears to be a chef. Out of work. He's proposing he be invited with the rest of the A-listers so he can network."

Lucie glanced up at Tim. "Spurned friend. Would he be mad enough for blackmail?"

"Maybe." Tim, in full detective mode, waggled a finger at the screen. "Print copies of all these. Please."

"Yeah. No problem."

"What about the IP address the ransom note was sent from?"

"Working on it. This particular provider hides the IP address. It's a privacy thing. I'll need some time."

"Fine. Keep at it. And see if you can find anything about the name on the account."

THE FOLLOWING MORNING, LUCIE SAT AT HER DESK ENJOYING the blissful quiet while Ro attended a meeting at their largest client.

Lucie adored Ro. Loved her beyond measure. Some mornings though, particularly after being accused of theft and blackmail, Lucie needed a drama-free zone. The minute Ro entered a room she brought a storm of energy with her. Sometimes it was too much.

Yes, time alone. Away from Hurricane Ro, away from Villa Rizzo and her father's daily questions about her life and business and whatever else entered his mind at 7:00 AM.

Lucie sat back, closed her eyes for a few seconds, taking in the hiss of the ancient radiator. When she was ten, her mom had brought her into this very shop for school shoes, and Lucie tripped on the rug and went head first into that radiator.

Joey still teased her about it.

And here she still was. Only, this time, the business—along with its reputation—belonged to her.

Leads. She needed to get back to researching the fire-fighters. And that friend of Antoine's who'd been snubbed from the party. Something about that nagged her.

An out-of-work chef probably needed money. Could he be angry enough to resort to blackmail? Over a party?

Who knew? Crazier things had happened in the world of Lucie Rizzo.

Her phone rang and she sat forward, checking the number. Dean, hacker/degenerate gambler.

"Hi, Dean. Please tell me you have news."

"Sort of. Your boyfriend, he's a cop, isn't he? He sounds like a cop. That's not good."

Certain information, Dean didn't need. More to protect Tim than anything. From the start of their relationship, Lucie had refused to put Tim's career in jeopardy.

"Tim's occupation doesn't matter. He's a safe zone," she said. Dean's silence lingered for a few seconds. "Dean, keep in mind we had a deal."

New career. Passive aggressive leg-breaking.

"I'm aware," he said. "Just clarifying what I suspected."

"Noted. What do you have for me?"

"I think the account the blackmailer sent that email from is fake. That's what I'd do. It's most likely a dead end."

Thanks for that cheery news. "Okay."

"But there are several emails between Antoine and the

angry chef. Antoine should choose his friends more carefully. This one's a complete ass."

"How so?"

"The friend is being sued. He was supposed to cater a wedding for an executive on the Gold Coast. The family rented a winery for an entire weekend and hired the chef for the rehearsal dinner and the wedding."

That had to be a decent paying gig. "What happened?"

"It doesn't say, but it looks like he never showed. He's being sued for breach of contract."

Whoa. Lucie sat back, staring at the garment rack loaded with samples behind Ro's desk. "So, not only is he unemployed, he's being sued. He needs money."

Given that lawsuits were made public, Lucie jotted a quick note to search online for the filing papers. "Does it say how much he's being sued for?"

"No. It'd be easy enough to find, though."

"I'll look into that. Thank you."

The doggie bells jangled. Lucie looked over and—*holy cannoli*—in walked Molly Jacardi, Antoine's girlfriend and manager.

What the heck would she be doing here? Molly nodded, but hovered in the doorway.

"Um, Dean, someone just walked in. Thank you for this information. Please keep me updated."

Lucie disconnected, then turned her attention to Molly. Under a long black coat, she wore black slacks and a white silk blouse with what looked like three long silver necklaces, all artfully layered around her neck. Edgy, yet elegant.

"Hi," Lucie croaked. *Damn it.* What did she have to be nervous about? She'd done nothing wrong. Still, Molly's visit—her first visit—to Coco Barknell after her client's world famous recipe had been stolen didn't bode well.

Lucie motioned to one of her guest chairs. "Have a seat."

"Thank you." The all-business voice.

Molly left her coat on, smoothing it under her legs as she sat, and casually hung her arms over the armrests.

Lucie's stomach flipped.

Something about Molly's crisp tone and relaxed body language, a cobra about to strike, set Lucie on edge. But, heck, she was Joe Rizzo's kid. She wouldn't be bullied.

"What can I help you with?"

"You know I'm a lawyer as well as Antoine's manager."

"I'm aware."

Molly glanced around the room, taking it all in, a small, condescending smile playing on her lips. "You understand that unless Antoine's recipe is returned, preferably today, I will have no problem putting you out of business. I will bring a media storm down on you that will make your little business crumble. You'll be lucky if you don't wind up in a jail cell. Of course, that's nothing new in your world, is it?"

Oh, this witch.

Lucie sat forward, meeting Molly's gaze. "There's one problem with your plan. I haven't done anything wrong."

"Last week you were late picking up Brie for her walk and she peed on a $30,000 rug. Destroyed it. The public relations aspect would be epic. How many of your wealthy clients would want to risk their beloved pet soiling expensive furniture?"

Evil! Her mother's voice echoed in her ear, reminding her that Rizzos stayed strong. *We don't sweat.* Trial after trial, the mantra stayed strong. "We were five minutes late due to a traffic accident on the next block. You think your media blitz will pummel us under those circumstances? In Chicago, where it takes twenty minutes to circle a block? I doubt it." Lucie drove her finger into her desktop. "I don't like you coming in here, insulting me or my family. I told Antoine and I'm telling you, I don't have that recipe. Plenty of people had access to that office after I left."

"But you were right there. All you'd need to do is snatch it from the safe."

"Which I didn't. And if you continue with this slander, I'll be forced to take legal action. Which, hmmm..." Lucie tapped her finger against her lips. "I recall Antoine saying he wanted to keep this out of the press. A slander lawsuit against the famous Chef Antoine would bring all sorts of questions, don't you think?"

Molly laughed. A genuine from-the-gut laugh reminiscent of the bad sixties horror movies Joey got a kick out of watching.

The door swung open, sending the doggie bells flying as Dad strode in for the first of his minimum six daily visits.

"Baby girl." He focused on her then stopped short, apparently seeing something he didn't like.

Lucie forced a smile, but her father was no slouch when it came to reading people. When it came to his children? Total ace.

"Hi, Dad."

"What's wrong?"

"Nothing. This is Molly Jacardi. We were actually just finishing up." Lucie turned her faux-cheery smile on Molly. "So good to see you. Thanks for coming by."

The not-so-subtle hint booted Molly out of the chair, her head high as if they'd just shared a lovely chat. Dad turned back and held the door open for her.

"Thank you," she said.

"You better not have been harassing my daughter."

Molly kept walking, distancing herself from *the* Joe Rizzo. So much for her threats. Everyone was all tough, insulting talk until they came face-to-face with the man himself.

Unbelievable.

Dad closed the door and jerked his thumb. "I don't like her. She's a looker, but it's a hard pretty. Baby girl, you can't trust hard pretty."

"She's an entertainment manager. She works for Chef Antoine."

"The recipe guy? The one who accused you of stealing?"

"Yes."

"Why was she here?"

The day after Lucie's twelfth birthday she'd lied to her father. Well, she'd attempted to lie. He suspected the lie and drilled her with a look that shattered her like Humpty Dumpty falling off his wall. After that, she'd never attempted to lie again, opting for truth and whatever consequences came her way.

"Well, Dad, she wanted to let me know that if I didn't return the recipe, they'd destroy my business."

"Again with that damned recipe?" Her father waved his hands. "That's it. I'm talking to this bum. We'll straighten this out."

That's all she needed. "Dad, no. I took care of it."

"How?"

She stood, walked to her father, and slung her arm through his. "Thank you for wanting to help. I may not deal with problems the same way you do, but I'm also Joe Rizzo's kid. I won't let anyone destroy my business without a fight."

———

"THAT BITCH."

Ro slammed her hand against Lucie's desk and

somehow her whole body shook. Boobs jiggled, hips swayed, head bobbed, all of it happening at once.

If Lucie had a nickel for every time Ro called someone a bitch, they wouldn't have to worry about expenses.

Lucie settled Dad down and installed him back at Petey's, the luncheonette that doubled as his office, only to have Ro return and submerge them into another round of rage control.

Hoping to halt the impending tirade, Lucie put her hands up. "Calm down before we have to put you in traction."

Ro flipped her hair over her shoulder, sending the long strands flying. Not a lot of people did haughty outrage on Ro's level.

"I wish I'd been here when all this went down. I haven't given anyone, aside from your idiot brother, a good piece of my mind in a long time. I have enough pent-up anger that I could do some damage."

Good to know.

An email dinged on Lucie's laptop and she forced herself not to look. Almost 11:00 and she hadn't crossed one thing from her daily to-do list. After the time spent chasing leads yesterday, this made two days' worth of tasks the president and CEO of Coco Barknell had fallen behind on.

Who had time to be accused of blackmail?

"This whole thing is crazy," Lucie said. "Am I the biggest magnet for bad luck there is?"

"Absolutely."

"Um, rhetorical question. But, hey, thanks for your honesty."

"Anytime." Ro speared a finger in the air. "Enough with the nonsense. What are we doing about this bitch? Do you want me to handle it?"

Uh, no. After Ro's most recent skirmish with the legal system due to the death of a reality star, Lucie didn't want her anywhere near Molly.

She pushed out of her chair, grabbed the file with her case notes, then crossed to Ro's desk, smacking the file down. "My notes on the case. All the leads and the latest from Dean the hacker."

Using her nail, Ro swept the folder open and perused Lucie's notes. "Ooh, this friend of Antoine's looks promising."

"Yes. Reuben LeBeau. I was about to start researching the lawsuit when Molly walked in. We need to know how much he's being sued for, who brought the suit, and what the status is. My thought is Antoine's friend, who happens to be out of work, needs fast cash."

Ro smacked her hand again. "Yes. Add that to him being upset over the lack of party invite and we may have a blackmailer."

Could it be that easy? "Don't get your hopes up."

"Why?"

"Would this guy be dumb enough to blackmail Antoine after admitting his troubles with finding work, a pending lawsuit and being mad over the party slight?"

"Why not? Where we come from, we've seen dumber criminals."

Lucie shrugged. "I agree, but I'm not sure I'm buying it. It's a lead and we should follow it. Would you look into that for me?"

"Where are you going?"

"I, my friend, am going to Molly's office."

Ro gasped. "Without me? You are no fun at all."

"Sorry, but this is a solo mission."

"Why?"

"Anna."

"The blonde? I hate how skinny she is. I used to be that skinny. Then I started dating your brother and your mother killed me with coffee cake. At least when I was getting divorced, I was thin."

"And miserable."

"Sacrifices, Luce. That's all."

Good old Ro. Always with the priorities. "Anna has been our main contact for Antoine's business. She handled getting the dog walking paperwork in order and tracking down that missing invoice for us."

"So?"

"So, maybe Anna can convince her boss that accusing innocent people of theft isn't exactly playing nice."

"What if she won't help?"

"Then we go to the mattresses."

Ro threw her hands up. "Yay. I love the mattresses."

USING HER FINELY HONED DETECTIVE SKILLS, LUCIE SAT IN HER car observing the comings and goings at Molly's office. She checked the time on her phone. 11:45. With any luck, Molly would head out. Antoine had once mentioned Molly spent her lunch hours at the yoga studio down the street. Stress reduction, she called it.

Whatever. As long as she got the heck out so Lucie could speak to Annalise without being interrupted.

At 11:50, the office door swung open and out came Molly, dressed in yoga pants, sneakers, and a long winter coat.

Heh, heh, heh.

Lucie waited for her to walk to the corner and turn right,

out of view. Even then, she waited another two minutes. Just to be sure.

Go time.

She strode into the office, expecting Molly's chipper receptionist.

Empty desk. She turned and peeked at the small waiting area and the unoccupied leather loveseat. A glass coffee table held three oversized books. One was Antoine's cookbook and the other two were photography books. Probably another client.

"Hello?" Lucie called.

Anna stepped into the hallway, spotted Lucie, and her mouth dipped into a frown. She paused, then cocked her head. "Lucie. Hi. Sorry. The receptionist is at lunch. I didn't hear you come in. Um, Molly isn't here."

Exactly my plan. "That's okay. I'm actually here to see you."

"Oh. Was there a problem with the invoice again?"

"No. That's all set. This is about Antoine and the missing recipe."

Anna clasped her hands in front of her, snuck a glance at her office, and pondered it for a long few seconds. Lucie's pulse hammered. Would she even be invited in?

Anna finally moved from her spot, walking toward Lucie.

No invitation to come inside. Fine. They'd do this standing in the entry.

"Of course," Anna said. "I'm not sure what I can do, though. You really should talk to Molly."

Anna stepped around her and marched toward the door, swinging it open. Oh, if only it were that easy to get rid of a Rizzo. The FBI had learned that the hard way.

Lucie eyed the door, then Anna, sending the clear

message she wasn't quite ready to leave. "I spoke to Molly this morning. She came to see me."

"*Really?*"

"Yes. She threatened to sue me. To tank my business."

Anna released the door, her fingers springing open as if they'd been singed. She let out a quiet sigh. "I'm sorry. Molly can be...tough."

No kidding. "I don't mind tough. But if she tries to ruin my reputation, I won't simply let it happen. I'll sue her for slander."

"Did you tell her that?"

"I did."

"That had to be an interesting conversation."

"It didn't end well." Lucie held out her hands. "Anna, we've always had a good working relationship. I feel horrible asking you this, but would you mind talking to her?"

Anna screwed up her face and her head shifted slowly. Back and forth, back and forth, back and forth.

Losing her. "I know it's a lot to ask, but it's in all of our interests for her to be reasonable. This *will* be resolved and when I'm cleared, I'd like us all to still have some sort of relationship. I'd be happy to help Antoine figure out who is behind this, but I'm not about to do that if Molly insists on slandering me or my business."

"Lawsuits won't help any of us."

"Exactly. Will you talk to her?"

Anna shook her head again, this time only once. Maybe there was hope here. She wasn't happy. Lucie saw that much in the hard line of her mouth. "Please, Anna. Anything you can do."

She stared at Lucie for a few seconds, the obvious war of

loyalty and reason raging. Loyalty was all fine...until it ruined someone.

Finally, Anna nodded. "I'll try. No promises, though. She'll think I betrayed her."

Success. A small bit anyway. "I understand. If you'd like my help, even on the sly, figuring out who is responsible, I'll help you. Anything to clear my name."

"I'm only doing this for Antoine. He's my client. *Our* client. I can't believe this is happening to him."

Finally, a reasonable person. "I know. It's horrible. I want you to know, I'm not the one doing this. I'm a business-woman. Plus, I've spent my life working to overcome the snickering that comes with my last name."

"I understand. Believe me. My dad died when I was ten. My mom never quite came out of it."

"I'm so sorry."

"Me too. Most people find a way to move on from the grief. Mom couldn't. She stayed in bed for months and I took care of all of us—my mom, brother and me. Making breakfast, packing lunches, getting us to the bus. I didn't realize how weird that was. It's all I knew." Anna stared off, out the window at the pedestrians on the sidewalk. The silence became a whoosh in Lucie's ears. Anna must have felt it, the odd tension. She faced Lucie again. "I learned from it, though. I never want to end up like my mom. So I get that whole making something of yourself. That's the only reason I'll talk to Molly."

In an odd way, they were both trying to rise above the legacy of their parent. The dysfunction in Anna's life made Dad look like a rock star. He had his faults, but he kept them fed and safe. She'd never condone his choice of employ-ment, but perhaps, once in a while, she could thank him for putting a roof over their heads and keeping shoes on their feet.

"Thank you, Anna. I was hoping you'd understand. Why would I want to risk all that I've built by doing something as stupid as stealing?"

———

ALL IN ALL, THE TALK WITH ANNA HAD GONE WELL. No promises, but she'd been reasonable. It gave Lucie hope that they'd straighten the mess out. Antoine would return as a client and, more importantly, maybe invest in the dog food company.

On her way to her car, Lucie fired up her phone. The voicemail alert chimed. And chimed. And chimed. Goodness, her phone was blowing up.

The phone rang. Ro's ringtone. Four calls and three texts. Overkill much? She hit the sidewalk and punched the answer button as she walked.

"Oh. My God!" Ro said. "Where are you?"

Lucie laughed. Couldn't help it. Dealing with a hyped-up Ro was better than a hit off a crack pipe. Assuming a hit off a crack pipe was good. "Just leaving my meeting with Anna. Why?"

"Meet me at McCormick Place."

"Why?"

"The chef."

"Antoine?"

"No. His friend. The broke-and-about-to-get-his-ass-sued one. He's got a one-day gig at a food show. They feature a different chef every half hour. It's open to the public."

Hmmm. Interesting. "And you know this how?"

"I followed him on Twitter. He posted it."

Very good. The drama queen definitely got points for that.

"And," Ro added, "let me just say, he is a *very*. Bad. Boy."

Lucie reached the corner and pressed the button to cross, her eyes focused on the electronic sign urging her not to walk. "What did he do?"

"I Googled him. He's had a few DUIs, a disturbing the peace charge, and an assault charge. The assault is sketchy. Looks like a bar fight. Lord, that's Joey every weekend. That one was dismissed, but he was later sued for damages. Medical bills and that. He's on the hook for $45,000."

That made two lawsuits, including the one pending from the wedding-gone-wrong.

"Huh," Lucie said. "He's a hot mess, isn't he?"

"You know it, girl. If you want to get a look at him, he'll be the featured chef at 1:30. I'm heading home now to change. I'll meet you there."

Leave it to Ro to waste time changing when the skirt and sweater she'd had on that morning were perfectly acceptable.

"Why are you changing?"

"Seriously? My work is never done. I need a button-down blouse in case we call in the troops."

8

"WHAT TIME IS IT?"

Lucie checked her phone while Ro messed with the exhibitor booth map, flipping it upside down and back again in a near-futile attempt to figure out where exactly they stood.

"It's 1:28 so we're good. He should just be starting."

"Yeah, but there are 500 exhibitors."

Just ahead of them, booths sat in clusters of four then extended into long rows. Lucie did a quick count of twenty rows.

Giant—gargantuan—room.

Ro angled back, checking the number above the door. "We are here." She pointed to the east entrance on the map then dragged her French-manicured fingernail to the west entrance. "Here's where we have to go. With this crowd, it could take an hour."

Once again, Lucie glanced at the crush of people monopolizing the rows.

"If we're getting through there, you'll need to do more than pop a few buttons."

"Sister, if it gets us through that mess, I'll strip to my skivvies. Just don't tell your brother."

Beep, beep. A balding man with enough liver spots on his head to draw a diagram honked at them from his motorized scooter. Lucie and Ro stepped aside.

"Sorry," Lucie said.

"Don't you worry, honey. Was just letting you know I'm coming through. My son is at the end of this aisle. He just invented some doohicky that pops lids off jars. Great for arthritis. Thought I'd come and support."

How sweet was that? Lucie smiled. "Well, good for you. Do you need help getting through the crowd?"

"Nah. I honk and if they don't move, I run their asses over."

Ro held her hands to the ceiling. "Sent straight from heaven. I simply adore him."

"Gotta be aggressive," the man said, "or you get swallowed up."

He hit the accelerator and zoomed by, almost taking out two women, who flipped him off.

Ro grabbed hold of Lucie. "Come on, we're hitching a ride on his tail."

Beep, beep. Beep, beep. "Coming through," the man hollered above the crowd.

"Make way," Lucie added.

The man swung a look back at her, nearly plowing over a woman carrying a huge box of pots.

"Watch it, old man!"

He swerved left around the woman, keeping Lucie and Ro with him.

"Hope you don't mind," Lucie said. "We're hitching a ride with you. We need to get to the west entrance lickety-split."

"Stick with me, honey, I'll get you there. Name is Sam, by the way."

"Hi, Sam. I'm Lucie and this is my friend Ro."

They neared the end of the row, narrowly escaping the wrath of no less than a dozen people, some using swear words Lucie had never even heard of.

"You're awesome, Sam," she said.

He gave them a thumbs-up. Lucie and Ro broke off, sprinting toward the west entrance. Well, as much as Ro could sprint in stilettos and a skin-tight leather skirt.

The aroma of cooking garlic mixed with...something... wafted toward them. "Smells good," Lucie said. "I'll need a snack after this."

"We're on a diet."

"We are?"

"If you're with me, yes. What you do on your own time is your business." Ro pointed. "I think this is him. I recognized him from the pictures online."

Lucie and Ro pushed toward the front of the small crowd surrounding the platform and inched to the second row. Ro nudged into an open space behind a woman no taller than Lucie.

With Ro's height, not to mention boobs, her presence would make itself known. Lucie had come to accept certain things about her childhood friend. One of those things being her BFF's ability to walk into a room, make eye contact with men and turn some of them to slobbering idiots.

Ro had outdone herself today in a leopard-print coat, the leather skirt, and a cream blouse with buttons begging for release.

Rueben LeBeau, a tall man with sandy blond hair and a

spotless chef's coat, wielded two frying pans, shaking and tossing vegetables.

"As you can see," he said, "the trick is to use a non-stick pan. Plus, it makes for easy cleanup. For those of you who just walked up, I'm preparing shrimp fried rice. A quick, satisfying meal the whole family will go for. You can do this with chicken, beef, or pork. Or all of the above. I experiment with vegetables, too. I love the versatility of this recipe. Need it to be gluten-free? No problem, just swap out the rice for a gluten-free alternative. I've done it today with a nice jasmine rice. It has a kick of sweetness to it."

He set the pans down, scanned his crowd, and tossed in more vegetables.

His eyes, of course, met Ro's and she offered up a flirty smile.

"Pop a button," Lucie said. "We need him to lock on."

"Look at you. Usually you're rolling your eyes."

"Usually I'm not accused of blackmail. Before this is over, I want this guy drooling and weak."

Ro reached up and casually opened another button on her shirt. "I got this, Luce. He's toast."

A man no less than one hundred shuffled up behind them, his veiny hand wrapped around a cane, slightly bumping Ro to make room for an equally veiny woman.

Giving him what little space she could, Ro stepped forward and found herself on the receiving end of a glare from the brunette in the front row.

"Sorry," Ro said. "Making room for the older folks coming in."

Then Lucie felt something brush her rear. *What the...* She peeped over her shoulder and the old man met her gaze with watery brown eyes. A filthy smile played on his lips.

Attempting to ignore him, Lucie refocused her mind to the matter at hand.

"Yip." Ro swung around, the purse hanging on her shoulder flying into the brunette. "Hey, old man, did you just squeeze my rear?"

"Quit pushing," the brunette said.

Ro gawked. "Well, *sor-ry*. I've got an ass-grabber here."

Terrific. On a mission and they run headlong into a pervert attracted to leopard print.

Lucie narrowed her eyes at the old man, who lifted his chin defiantly.

"Wilbur, did she say something?" his wife asked, her voice loud and carrying above the crowd.

Apparently, the missus left her hearing aids at home.

Ro waggled a finger. "Keep your hands to yourself. I have no problem decking handsy men. I don't care how old you are."

"All right, folks!" The chef's voice boomed through the speakers as he fought to regain the attention of the crowd. "The vegetables are cooking. Let's crack an egg in here and scramble that."

He made eye contact with Ro again and she dipped her head, placing her hand over her heart. The sex-kitten form of apology. Lucie nearly gagged, but the chef? He blew her a kiss.

Blech.

"Lord," Lucie said.

"Wilbur?" the old woman said again.

"There, there, Mavis. Everything is fine."

But the woman's eyes burned into Ro. "Whore!"

Whoa.

Ro's face contorted, her skin stretching into a long, open-mouthed gape.

If this woman hadn't been a million years old, Ro would have cold-cocked her—*bam*—and sent her to the floor.

Geriatric insults were tough. Even Ro wasn't mean enough to hit a woman older than dirt.

Lucie might be, though. Calling someone a whore in a crowded area was just wrong.

"Ma'am," Lucie said, "apologize to my friend. That's not nice."

The woman raised her open hand to the ceiling. "Marriage," she said, her voice overtaking Chef Reuben's, "is honorable in all, and the bed undefiled: but whoremongers and adulterers God will judge!"

Ro snapped from her stupor. "Did she just call me a *whoremonger*?"

"These shall hate the whore," the woman droned on, "and shall make her desolate and naked, and shall eat her flesh, and burn her with fire."

The brunette in the front row turned back. "That one I recognize. Book of Revelation."

"Shrimp is in," the chef said.

God, this was a freak show. A growing one. The crowd behind them had doubled. More than likely from the preaching about whores and adulterers.

The old woman's eyes seared into Ro. "For true and righteous are his judgments: for he hath judged the great whore, which did corrupt the earth with her fornication."

The woman in front elbowed her friend. "That's definitely Revelation."

Outrage flooded Lucie. How dare these people judge them? "She's insulting my friend. How is it our fault this woman's husband is an ass-grabber?" Lucie whirled on the older couple. "You should both be ashamed of yourselves.

You, sir, for being a pervert. And you, ma'am, for enabling his horrid behavior. Now, apologize to my friend."

From the podium, Reuben cleared his throat. "Let's mix it all up!"

"Oh, I'll mix it up, all right," Ro said.

Someone nudged from behind, knocking the old woman into Lucie and Lucie into the friend of the woman playing bible trivia.

The woman stumbled forward. Lucie reached for her, hoping to keep her from going over.

"Hey," the friend yelled, gripping the back of Lucie's coat and shoving her.

"Now I'm done," Ro said.

Oh, no.

Visions of a bloody Tiffy Nelson sprawled on the playground blacktop filled Lucie's mind. Back then, Ro caught an in-school suspension. Now? If she clubbed someone, she'd wind up slapped with an assault charge.

Can't have that.

Lucie leaped in front of Ro, body blocking her. Undeterred, Ro poked a finger at the woman. "Touch my friend again," she said, "and I'll knock you out."

"Chick fight," someone from the back yelled.

"And here we are," Chef said, "a nice family meal. Finish it with soy sauce and it's a crowd pleaser."

Could he still be cooking?

Lucie glanced up, found him holding a giant bowl of fried rice for the crowd to see.

"Who wants a taste test?" he asked

The crowd let up a cheer and everyone pushed around Ro, Lucie, and the smackdown about to ensue.

Two women in black skirts, crisp white shirts, and bow ties stepped from behind a screen. They each carried a giant tray of samples, drawing the crowd to the end of the small stage.

Chef hopped off the platform and landed beside Lucie. "Ladies, what's the problem?"

"Ask that ass-grabbing old man," Ro said. "Where is that little filth ball?"

"This bitch pushed my friend," the woman with the brunette said.

"Because someone pushed me," Lucie cried. "I only grabbed her to keep her from falling."

"And don't call Lucie a bitch."

Chef held up his hands. "Ladies, if I may." He gave them a little bow that was equal parts cheesy and charming. "The drama provided a nice crowd, and I'm forever grateful, but let's not have security show up."

Ro tossed her hair back. "It's all the ass-grabber's fault."

Where'd they go? Lucie scanned the crowd, found the couple moving toward the samples, and sighed.

"Unbelievable. They cause a brawl and then scoot off."

"Come on," the brunette said. "Did he seriously cop a feel?"

Ro held up a hand. "I swear he did."

The brunette shook her head. "And this from a God-fearing man. I've seen it all."

"Look," Ro said, "I apologize for bumping you. You were collateral damage. Couldn't be helped."

The woman waved her off. "Eh. It's fine. I don't blame you for being mad." She turned to her friend. "Let's go, Mo. I hear there's pulled pork at this end of this aisle."

The two women cut around the crowd gobbling up the fried rice, but Chef Reuben still stood beside Ro and Lucie.

Might as well capitalize on it. She eyed Ro. The roll-with-me stare.

"Chef," she held out her hand. "I'm Lucie. I am so sorry we ruined your demonstration."

His face lit up. "Are you kidding? Look at this crowd. I beat the guy before me by at least twenty people."

Competition. Always a motivator.

"The rice smells fantastic."

"Hold on. You have to try it."

He hopped back onto the stage, scooped some rice into a smaller bowl and handed it down to Lucie with a couple of forks.

"Go ahead. Please."

The two of them dug in. Chef's gaze ping-ponged between them, as if waiting for a reaction. A sigh, a moan, any indication of orgasmic pleasure.

"Fabulous," Ro said. "Is the soy sauce homemade?"

"It is. My secret recipe." He winked at Ro. "You have to get the salt just right."

If this guy was a blackmailer, he played it down like a Hollywood A-lister. Nothing in his mannerisms said *crook*. If anything, Lucie sensed immense pride in his work.

Lucie met Ro's eyes again. With time dwindling before the ransom drop, they needed to start eliminating suspects.

"You know," Lucie said, "we're here today to scope out potential caterers."

"Really?"

Lucie nodded.

"What type of an event?"

Uh...

"Wedding," Ro blurted.

Rueben smiled. "A wedding. Excellent. My specialty."

Lawsuit notwithstanding.

"Which one of you is the lucky girl?"

"Her."

"Her."

Chef's eyebrows drew together.

"Double wedding," Lucie said.

Good God. *Totally off script here.*

"Fun," he said. "How big of a crowd?"

Yikes-a-roo with all the questions. Who knew hiring a caterer required so many details? Lucie reminded herself this man was out of work. Having been downsized before, she understood the panic and heartbreak that came with being unemployed. Even to find a blackmailer, she wouldn't give false hope.

"We're still working that out. We're trying to decide if we want to go with a traditional venue that will handle the food or something a little different."

"Like what?"

Silence drifted. Lucie sent a help-me signal to her BFF.

"Um," Ro said, "my aunt's mansion. In Barrington."

Ro moving on the fly. Excellent work.

"Lovely," Chef said.

An aha-moment fired Lucie's brain. A man blackmailing his friend for two million dollars would probably want to be available at the time of the ransom drop. If Reuben was available at 11:00 the next morning, they might be able to eliminate him from the suspect list.

"Yes," Lucie said. "We're actually meeting with potential caterers tomorrow. Are you familiar with Chef Antoine Durand? His casserole is to die for."

Reuben blanched, but she'd give him credit for cementing his charm-boy smile in place.

"Antoine? Of course. He's actually an acquaintance. We worked together when we were both straight out of school. Excellent chef." He winked at Lucie. "Obviously, I'd tell you

I'm better, but we can leave that to you to decide. I'd love to prepare a meal for you to prove it."

Beside Lucie, Ro cocked her head. "How I do love a man with confidence."

"My work speaks for itself. As does Antoine's."

"But you're better," Ro said.

He met her eye, holding the contact a beat longer than necessary. "Without a doubt. In fact, in the healthy spirit of competition, why don't you have us each prepare the same meal for you? A tasting before you make a decision."

A cocky little bugger, but clearly he wasn't afraid to pit his culinary skills against the great Antoine.

Which, in Lucie's humble opinion, was what this was about. Taking on the more famous and wealthier chef.

And winning.

How very interesting.

Lucie nodded. "That's an idea if we decide to go with a private chef. I don't want to mislead you, but if you're available tomorrow, maybe we could discuss some possibilities."

"What time?"

"Say, around *eleven*."

Ro coughed, then smacked herself on the chest. "Wow. Sorry. Got a tickle."

Yes, I know what I'm doing.

Rueben, plucked his phone from his back pocket. "I think that should be fine." He tapped the screen then scrolled. "Yep. My morning is clear."

Dang it.

"Excellent," she said, her voice heavy on the fake cheer.

He reached back to the table for a stack of business cards. "Here's my card. My business manager's name is on the back. If we move forward, she'll be handling the contracts."

"Sounds perfect. Thank you. I'll call you later to confirm."

Chef glanced over Lucie's shoulder at the small crowd still cooing over his rice. "Ladies, lovely talking to you, but I need to go."

He wandered off and Lucie read the card he'd given her. A nice white card with embossed lettering and a chef's hat logo. Cute. She flipped the card over. "No way."

"What is it?"

"His business manager."

"What about him?"

Lucie held the back of the card up. "Her. It's Molly Jacardi. Same as Chef Antoine."

THOUGHTS STILL CIRCLING THE POSSIBLE IMPLICATIONS OF Molly managing Reuben LeBeau, Lucie came to a stop and double-parked in front of Villa Rizzo. She hopped out to move the ancient lawn chair Dad had left—so thoughtful—in the Rizzo *reserved* spot.

In her lifetime, Lucie couldn't recall one instance where someone had moved the chair and commandeered the space. Maybe it was fear of Joe Rizzo's wrath or simply a sense of honor. Certain things in this neighborhood were sacred. Reserved spots were one of them.

Particularly in the winter. If you dug snow out of a parking space, you basically owned it until the snow melted.

Lucie parked, locked the car, and grabbed her briefcase from under the blanket she kept in her backseat to hide things under.

Waning sunlight dipped below the rooflines, taking

precious heat with it. This time of year, they were lucky to even have sunlight at 4:30 in the afternoon.

Her phone rang. Tim returning her call. She'd called him from the office to update him that her background checks on the firefighters were a dead loss. Not one of those people appeared to be doing anything fishy. Damn them.

Not good with the ransom drop looming.

Who knew if Antoine even had the money together?

Dean. She'd check with him. See if there might be emails regarding money movement.

"Hello, Detective," she said into the phone.

"Hello, Ms. Rizzo."

Their silly little name game brought a sense of calm to Lucie's otherwise lagging nervous system. *Tick-tock, tick-tock.*

She stepped onto the curb, inhaled a long pull of crisp winter air, and let the cold center her. "Listen, hot stuff, I'm halfway through the list of firefighters. I've spent a small fortune paying for background checks. They're all clean. Barely a parking ticket."

"It was worth checking them out. My buddy has a sister who's a paramedic. I'll ask if she knows any of them. What was the other message you left me? About the chef."

"The friend. He was doing a demo today at a food show, so Ro and I went to check it out. And before you get all mad about my screwball investigations, you should know it was a bust."

"What happened?"

"Aside from Ro being called a whore by a bible thumper with a perv of a husband?"

Tim let out a strangled laugh. "Excuse me?"

"I'll tell you about it later. Needless to say, it got the chef's attention. We talked to him after the demo and made up some nonsense about wanting him to cater a wedding. A double wedding."

Silence.

A chunk of Lucie's heart might have been sheared clear off by its sharpness. The horrifying thought of marrying her rendered him speechless.

Shake it off.

"Relax, Tim. He caught us off guard and Ro ran with it. We weren't being serious. Sorry if I terrified you."

Because, after all, why would the honorable Tim O'Brien even want to marry into the Rizzo family? After what he'd seen of her life, he should run.

Fast.

"Luce, you didn't terrify me. Well, the whole double wedding thing with Joey and Ro, maybe. But you. Never. I love you."

Did that mean...

No. She couldn't go there now. Not the time. They'd never talked next steps and certainly never marriage.

Maybe that chunk of her sheared off heart didn't hurt so bad.

"I love you, too. Thank you. That means a lot to me. Anyway, I floated the idea of the chef meeting us tomorrow at 11:00 to discuss catering options. He didn't flinch."

"Oooh. Might not be our guy. But you never know. Could be someone else picking up the money."

"It gets better. Guess who his business manager is?"

"Who?"

"Molly Jacardi. Chef Antoine's Molly."

Silence again. Lucie checked the bars on her phone.

"Interesting," Tim said.

"I know. I may ask Dean to search Antoine's emails and see if there's any mention of Molly and Reuben."

And look at her talking hackers with her cop boyfriend. What a life.

"Ms. Rizzo?"

Lucie swung around. A tall man in a cheap, ill-fitting suit walked toward her. Niggling apprehension skittered up her neck.

"Lucie Rizzo?"

"Yes."

"Who's that?" Tim wanted to know.

"No idea," Lucie said. "A guy in a suit. Hold on."

She kept the phone to her ear, making sure to let the man know if he intended on killing her in front of her mob boss father's house, the person on the other end of her phone call would hear it.

On cue, the front door swung open and Dad stepped onto the porch.

As much as she didn't want to admit it—she was a grown up for God's sake—her father's protective presence steadied her.

"Baby girl?"

"Hi, Dad." She faced the guy in the suit. "Can I help you?"

He shoved an envelope at her. "You've been served."

"They're suing me! So much for Anna's help."

Still talking to Tim, Lucie smacked the summons on the coffee table and collapsed onto the couch.

"For what?"

"Everything." She sat up, found the paragraph outlining the complaint. "We have—and I'm paraphrasing here—

breach of contract, personal property damage, mental hardship."

"Mental hardship? What's that about?"

"According to this, Brie suffered because she had to pee so bad."

Tim, her beloved, laughed. So maddening.

"I'm about to lose my business and you think it's funny? I'm not joking. It says it right here. Mental hardship. On the dog."

Dad wandered over, picked up the summons, and skimmed it. His lips puckered as he read. "Frivolous lawsuit. It'll get thrown out."

"He's right," Tim said, clearly overhearing her father's comment.

A Chicago cop agreeing with her father. Amazing.

Lucie held the phone to her ear, but looked up at her father. Two birds. One stone. "That's not the point. With Antoine as the plaintiff, the media will be all over this. Molly is already feeding it to the press. I need a lawyer. Tim, I'll call you back."

"This," Dad said, "is a new one. Got the best criminal lawyer in the state on retainer and he's no damned good on a civil case."

Well, she could start with him. She found Willie's number and punched him up.

He answered on the first ring. "What now?"

Sarcasm. Great. She was surrounded by smart asses. "You lucked out this time. It's not criminal. Do you know a good civil attorney?"

"Why?"

"I'm being sued because a dog peed on his owner's $30,000 rug."

Willie huffed. Nobody did subtle outrage like Willie

Clay. "Who pays thirty grand for a rug and lets a dog walk on it?"

Dad waggled a hand. "What's he saying?"

Lucie glanced up. "He's in awe that someone paid $30,000 for a rug."

"No foolin' there."

"I know someone," Willie said. "Give me two minutes."

The front door opened. Joey and Mom walked in carrying the reusable shopping totes Mom favored.

She held up the green one. "Bone-in ribeyes for dinner. Joey said he'd even light the grill so we can cook them outside. I love barbecuing in the winter."

Joey took one look at Lucie and halted. The energy in the room must have put his uh-oh senses on full alert. "What now?"

Another one with the smart-ass comment. As if she asked for this kind of trouble?

Dad waved one hand. "Your sister is being sued by a wackadoo."

"For what?"

Lucie's phone rang. "This is Willie again. Fill Joey in while I talk." She poked the screen. "Hi, Willie."

"Get a pen and paper."

"Great. Hold on."

She put the phone on speaker, set it down, and flipped open her messenger bag for her legal pad.

A white sheet of paper sat in front of the legal pad. Hmmm. She didn't remember putting anything in there. And, being an A-type, she certainly wouldn't just shove it in there where it could get wrinkled. She'd put it in a folder first.

Another bout of that neck prickling apprehension fired. *What is it?* She slid the paper out and...

"Come on!"

"What *now*?"

She shoved the page at Joey and flopped backward on the couch, her hands on top of her head.

Joey held the page up. "I guess we just found the missing recipe."

LUCIE STARED AT THE RECIPE IN HER BROTHER'S HAND wondering—in the words of the great Joey Rizzo—WTF?

She shook her head and blinked back an onslaught of emotion that made her eyes well up. "I don't understand what's happening here. I did *not* steal that recipe."

From his end of the phone, Willie perked up. "Stealing?"

He was happy. Every Rizzo incident increased the size of his checkbook.

Joey waved her off. "We know *you* didn't do it. You think we'd believe Miss Goodie-Two-Shoes would do that?"

Compliments. Rizzo style. "Thank you."

"Besides, even if you did swipe it, you wouldn't be dumb enough to leave it in your briefcase." He circled around the sofa and picked up Lucie's phone. "Willie, we'll call you back if we need you. Stand by."

Dad ripped the page from Joey, waving it around as his face turned the weird shade of purple that preceded a tantrum. "I wanna know who setup my baby girl."

"Here we go," Joey said. "Dad, relax. Before you give yourself a coronary."

Mom poked her head into the dining room from the kitchen. "What's all the yelling about?"

"Frame-up on our baby girl."

Now Mom was on the move, storming through the dining room toward Lucie. "What frame-up?"

Dad picked up the cordless phone.

"Not the cordless," Joey said. "Cell phone."

"You're right. I keep forgetting."

Suspicious that the feds had tapped the house phone, Dad had taken to using his cell for certain calls. Certain calls that might get him locked up on a parole violation.

Joey handed his phone to Dad. "Who're you calling?"

"The boys. I'm putting everyone on this. We're gonna find out who planted that recipe."

Mom watched the exchange between Dad and Joey then swiveled to Lucie. "What frame-up?"

"I found Antoine's missing recipe in my briefcase."

"No."

"Yes."

Banner day all around. All these years she'd strived to lead a good, honest life.

Something had to change. She couldn't keep doing this. Keep fighting against the Rizzo reputation. The more she fought, the more she wound up in hinky situations that stressed her out.

Well, maybe she needed to stop fighting. Just let people think what they'd think and live her life, reputation be damned.

Her phone rang. Tim's ringtone. *Lordy.* She'd told him she'd call him back and hadn't. He must have been frantic. She picked up the phone. "Hi."

"Are you okay?"

"I am. Sorry about that. It got crazy around here."

And, by the way, someone is setting me up.

She couldn't do it. Couldn't tell him. Not over the phone and not until she wrapped her mind around it. How many of these situations could she put this man through before he gave up on her?

"I'm in the middle of a case, but I can swing by for a few minutes. Do you need me?"

Always.

"No. It's okay. Right now there's nothing you can do. Willie gave me a civil lawyer to call. I was just about to do that. I'll call you when I know something."

"Are you sure? You sound...weird."

"Just another day in paradise."

"I'm sorry. The lawsuit is dumb. We can fight that, Luce. It's leverage and it won't work."

The recipe in her briefcase might though.

She inhaled a long, slow breath, let Tim's words sink in. When he said it, she almost believed it.

Enough with the misery. Misery wouldn't get her anywhere. She lifted her chin and pushed her shoulders back. Rizzos, for all their faults, weren't quitters.

Or whiners.

"You know what, Tim O'Brien? You're right. We've faced way worse than this. All I have to do is figure out how to back them off."

"That's my girl."

His girl. Damned straight.

"Thank you," she said.

"For what?"

"For reminding me who I am."

"I love you, Luce. Whatever you need, I'm here for you."

"I know." She glanced up at her parents and Joey

pretending they weren't eavesdropping. Well, they'd love this one. "I love you, too."

There. Said it. If they hadn't figured it out after all these months and family dinners, they knew now that she loved a hunky Irish cop.

Lucie disconnected and got to her feet. "Okay," she said, "we need a plan."

AFTER CALLING RO AND WAITING FOR JIMMY, SLIP, AND Lemon to show up, Lucie assembled everyone around the dining room table with one of Mom's famous coffee cakes and an assurance from Joey that he'd swept the house for bugs.

Since Dad's return home, he'd been upping his sweeps, just in case.

"We'd better eat the cake fast," Mom said. "Before Ro shows up and shuts us down. She's no fun when she's on a diet."

True. "We can eat and talk at the same time. Ro can catch up."

Joey waved a fork. "How'd someone get a hold of your briefcase?"

Question of the hour. "I left it in my car when I was downtown earlier. When I got back to the office, I just put the briefcase next to my desk like I always do. The recipe could have been in there the whole time."

Dad nodded. "They're sending a message. If they got in your car, they're watching you."

"And," Lemon said, "who knows where else they hid copies."

Lucie gawked. "You think there's more?"

"If it were me"—he held up his hand—"not saying I've ever done this, but I'd put more around. Maybe in your house or your desk."

Fighting her growing panic, Lucie pondered all the places a recipe could be hidden. Office, bedroom, Tim's house. *Oy.* "I don't think it would be in here. They'd be crazy to try it. The office though, I don't know. People come in and out during the day. Ro and I were downtown today and had a temp covering the phones."

Lucie made a note to ask the temp if anyone had come inside the shop.

"I'll do a more thorough search of my car and the shop." For kicks, she'd check her bedroom just to make sure.

The front door flew open. In came Ro, still wearing her whore-mongering leopard print coat and leather skirt.

"Hello, Rizzos." She spotted Dad's cronies. "And company."

Joey gave her his usual Joey look. The quasi pissed-off/bored one that instilled terror on half of Franklin. "Where you been?"

Ro strutted toward him, smacked him on the back of the head, and then kissed him. Strangest love language ever, but it worked.

"I had a few stops to make in town. In case you forgot, your sister and I are running a business. We have customers to keep happy." She perused the remaining coffee cake. "Cake before dinner? You people have lost your minds."

"We wanted to do it before you got here," Mom said. "You get cranky."

"Correction. My ass gets cranky."

Dad laughed. "She's got a filthy mouth, but I love her."

The house phone rang and Mom hopped up, taking the remaining coffee cake with her before Ro flew into some kind of sugar-restricted tirade. The phone ringing stopped and Lucie heard Mom say hello to Iris, the neighbor. Ninety-three years old and still living alone. God bless her. Mom helped out a lot. And even Joey. He'd take Iris to the grocery store a couple times a week just to get her out of the house. In Franklin, people took care of their neighbors.

Using great care—most likely to avoid popping a seam — Ro slid into the vacant chair next to Joey. "What's this meeting about?"

Lucie held up the summons. "We're being sued by Antoine. And I just found a copy of his recipe in my briefcase."

A long gasp of air exploded from Ro's mouth.

"Yep," Lucie said. "We're strategizing how to prove I didn't take that damned recipe. If we do that, this whole lawsuit goes away. And, tick-tock, because we're supposed to have a ransom drop tomorrow."

Mom popped her head back in. "I have to go next door. Iris dropped one of her anti-psychotic pills and she can't find it. She's afraid the cat will eat it."

Lucie had long since given up correcting her mother about Iris' anti-anxiety meds. What was the point?

A minute later, the back door closed and Joey waggled a hand. "It's good that she's gone. We can talk now."

Joey liked to protect their mother from all things criminal. Even Lucie's so-called screwball investigations.

"I think," Lucie said, "we should follow up on Molly managing Reuben. Am I the only one who thinks that's odd? Especially since he didn't get invited to Antoine's party. Molly would have seen that as an opportunity for him to mingle with high-rollers and potential employers."

Joey sat back, his big body making Grandma Rizzo's antique chair squeak. "Brace yourselves, but I'm gonna agree with Luce. Not that it's weird that this Molly broad handles the chef, but that we should take a look at her. I mean, we're not getting anywhere with the firefighters, right?"

"No. The background checks all came back clean. Aside from that, I'm not sure where to start with them. I want to at least give Molly a cursory look."

"Awright," Joey said. "What's your plan?"

"The obvious thought is to get into her office and look around."

"True," Ro said. "We should go over there. Talk to her about this crazy lawsuit and snoop."

"And how are we supposed to search her office with her in there?"

Ro let out a huff. "My work is never done. We'll create a distraction or something, I don't know. We just need to get her out of the office."

Not a bad thought, but that would give them what? Five minutes? To snoop around an entire office? Too little time.

Dad made a humming noise. "What you do is wait for her to leave."

This is what growing up with criminals got her. "As in break into her office?"

Dad shrugged.

"Dad! I'm not doing that. Snooping is one thing, breaking and entering? *Not* happening."

Tim would have a fit. And she wouldn't risk that. Nothing was worth losing him over.

"Ho," Jimmy said, "We should get those pain in the ass agents surveilling *us* to go in there. *That's* the way to do it."

Lemon backhanded Jimmy on the arm. "Remember when those bastards played like they were from the cable company and talked their way into your house?"

Joey cocked his head. "I never heard this. What happened?"

"Eh. It was years ago. Somethin' went screwy with my cable. My wife called and they said they'd send someone out. I leave the house and right away the guy shows up. He walks around, goes into the basement and does his thing. He can't figure it out. Tells my wife he'll send someone else. An hour later another guy shows up and he gets it fixed. No problem."

"Tell me," Joey said, "the first guy was a fed planting a bug."

"Yep."

"How'd you find it?"

Dad raised his hand. "After I got acquitted the second time, I got cautious."

Oh, please. Cautious didn't cover it. Back then her father had been downright paranoid. The stress level in Villa Rizzo had been insane. If Mom opened the drapes, Dad would close them. They had lived like shut-ins, rarely going out to dinner or to movies or any place where someone might have the opportunity to bug the house. Dad walked around speaking with his hand over his mouth because he was afraid lip readers were spying on him. That was a crazy year before the government finally hit pay dirt and nailed Dad on a tax charge that earned him two years in the clink.

"Cautious how?" Ro asked.

Jimmy looked at her over the rim of his glasses. "He hired someone to come in and sweep our houses for bugs every week."

Joey grinned at Dad. "Your guy found the bug?"

"Why do you think I had *you* start sweeping the house after I went away?"

"Huh," Joey said, his voice packing a whole lot of wonder. "I never knew that."

"You didn't need to know."

And there it was, their father, the puppeteer, allowing people to have only the information they needed. Was it fair? Who knew. He never shared his business with Lucie. Never. Joey? Parts of it, but Dad had been clear, Joey wouldn't have an active role in *the life*. Being a bookie was one thing. Becoming a mob guy? Dad wouldn't have it.

In his own twisted way, he wanted different—better even —for Joey.

Ro smoothed a wrinkle on the sleeve of her blouse. "Too bad Molly knows me. I'd make a great fed."

That revelation left the meeting occupants in a stunned, hanging silence.

Ro gave each of them the stink-eye. "You think I couldn't do it?"

"You don't exactly blend," Joey said.

Before this turned into one of their knockdown arguments, Lucie held up her hands. "Pretty sure posing as a federal agent is a crime."

"Hang on," Joey said.

No hang on. *Nuh-uh*. Hang on, with this particular bunch, meant nuttiness that might get someone confined to a penitentiary.

Her brother sat staring at the wall, his eyes a little squinty as he mulled something over.

Nothing but trouble to be had there. "Let's go back to the distraction idea," Lucie said. "We'll try to meet with Molly and get her out of the office. Definitely the safer way to go."

"No," Joey said. "I'll do it."

Wha...

Everyone swiveled toward him.

"We've got this," he said. "One of the cable guys comes into Petey's all the time for lunch. He wears his employee ID around his neck. We'll mock one up on the computer, put it in one of those lanyard things. I'll park myself outside this Molly's office and wait 'til she leaves. Then, boom." Joey clapped his hands. "I walk in there, tell them we have to check their wiring."

Lucie shook her head. "Not a good idea. If you get caught—"

"If I get caught, I'll leave. Are they going to arrest me for impersonating a cable guy?"

"There's a reality show for ya," Lemon cracked. "Joey the Cable Guy."

Ro did jazz hands. "Ooh, we should put a video camera on him—like the SEALs use on missions so the president can watch. We'll be able to see everything."

Dad pointed at her. "I like it."

Oh. My. God. "No. We're not doing that."

"Baby girl, think like the government. It's not a crime when it comes to law enforcement. If this broad is rotten, she needs to be dealt with. Consider it your civic duty. You'll be doing America a favor."

Joe Rizzo, law professor.

Roseanne nodded. "He's right, Luce. You said yourself we're running out of leads. This will be one more lead to check off our list. Joey is smart. If he gets in there and things don't feel right, he'll leave. No harm, no foul."

"I like it," Dad said. "I've always told your brother to watch out for you. And, no offense, baby girl, lately"—Dad motioned like he was turning a screw—"you've needed a lot of help. You didn't see my last bill from Willie."

"Don't start, Dad. I said I'd pay it."

"Cripes," Joey said, "here we go with the Miss-High-and-

Mighty routine. Look, I'm doing this. I don't care what you say. It's not just about you. Ro is a partner in Coco Barknell. Any lawsuit against you affects her."

Lucie sat back, the air—or maybe the fight—leaving her body. *They'll do it anyway.*

They would. Rizzos, including her, had been taught to never, ever give up. Whether it was a crossword puzzle, building a business, beating a criminal case, no matter what it took, they battled on. Even if it meant winding up a bloody stump.

That's what tunnel vision did—it messed with the mind and justified any action as long as they persevered.

Tick-tock. That ransom drop neared. Once Antoine paid the money, if that's what he still intended, he'd be out millions and still think she'd perpetrated the scheme.

Can't have that.

Lucie pushed out of the chair. "The only way to get rid of this lawsuit is to prove I'm innocent." She met Joey's eye. "Let's do it. But if you get caught, I'm taking the fall. I'll tell them it was all my idea."

"I won't get caught. Believe me."

LUCIE AND RO SAT IN THE FRONT SEAT OF RO'S GIANT Escalade, while Joey made his way down the block to Molly Jacardi's office. They'd dropped Joey off around the corner just in case someone spotted the big lug getting out of an SUV rather than a vehicle provided by the cable company. Now they sat across the street from Molly's office watching the activity.

"Testing, one, two, three," Joey said.

"Roger that," Ro said into the microphone on her headset.

First the spy electronics and now military lingo?

Lord. What were they doing?

Some quick research to the cable company's website verified the uniform of khaki pants and a red golf shirt with the company's logo. Ro downloaded the logo from the company website and with the help of Coco Barknell's commercial embroidery machine, *voila*, Joey the Cable Guy.

More importantly, he wore clear, dark rimmed eyeglasses —fake lenses—with a video camera tucked into the bridge. They'd purchased said glasses at the spy shop downtown. Lucie was once again amazed at the litany of scary things that could be purchased by walking into a retail store. She'd never look at anyone wearing eyeglasses without wondering…

A foul odor filled the car. Lucie whirled to see Sonny, Jimmy's crazy Jack Russell, snoozing on the back seat. Sonny was their plan B. If Joey got into trouble, Lucie would walk in with Sonny, using the excuse of being in the neighborhood walking a client, and request to speak with Molly.

Half-assed plan, for sure, but it would distract Molly's employees and hopefully allow Joey to sneak out the back door.

"That animal has the worst gas," Ro said.

"This is nuts."

"Well, sister, if you have a better idea, let's hear it."

Lucie watched as her brother strode through the door of the one-story brick building with large windows on either side of the entrance. Sickness welled in her stomach and she breathed in. How could she let her brother risk this for her? Was impersonating a cable guy a crime?

Should have researched that.

"I shouldn't let him do this."

"As if you'd be able to talk him out of it? You know what a Neanderthal he is. He loves you. He loves me, too. This is his way of taking care of us."

Lucie tilted her head, puckering her lips as she considered options.

"Hi," Joey's voice burst through her headset. Lucie focused on the iPad screen Ro held between them. Her brother stood in front of the receptionist's desk inside Molly's office. They couldn't see him, but had a visual of everything in his sightline.

"Hello," the receptionist said. "Can I help you?"

"I'm from the cable company. We're upgrading the lines and I need to swap out some hardware."

The receptionist peered straight ahead. Probably at Joey's doctored ID.

"Ro, if she looks too close..."

Joey glanced down, giving Lucie and Ro a clear view when he shifted his tool bag to his other hand and *accidentally* flipped the ID over.

"He's so good," Ro said.

But was that anything to be proud of?

Americans will thank you. Funny how something so twisted and illogical could justify their actions. Particularly when it came from Dad.

Intellectually, Lucie knew better. Emotionally? *Not so much.*

Onscreen, the young receptionist rose from her chair and waved Joey down the corridor leading to the offices and conference room. Her heels clicked against the hand-carved hardwood as Joey followed her, his gaze drifting south.

South to the young woman's butt firmly encased in fitted slacks.

Ro let out a long sigh. "Joey, you'd better not be checking out that girl's rear."

And, *whoopsie*, Joey's head snapped back up.

"Animal," Ro muttered. "This is what happens when you let men off-leash."

Joey snorted and the receptionist glanced over her shoulder. "One of our employees is using the conference room. You can start in her office or this first one."

Lucie, having picked up Brie at Molly's office one time, spoke into her headset. "First one. That's Molly's office."

Joey stopped, jerked a thumb. "I can start in here and make my way down."

The receptionist paused and swung back. "Okay. How long do you think you'll be?"

"Not long. Thirty or forty minutes."

The receptionist glanced toward the front, then to Molly's office, clearly deciding how to handle the big guy with the fake ID that she didn't know was fake. "All right. I can't leave the phones, but I'll come back and check on you."

Ro let out a huff. "He's the cable man for God's sake, not a thief."

"Technically, with what we're doing, he's a thief."

"You know what I mean."

The receptionist pushed open the door to Molly's office and left Joey standing in the hallway.

"Here we go," Joey said.

He stepped in, quickly scanning an office that should have been featured in a magazine. Slick, glossy, and insanely neat.

Coming from Lucie, who prided herself on being organized, that was saying something.

Keeping her gaze on the office's front entrance,

Lucie nodded. "Good. Don't dawdle. Find the cable outlet in case she comes back. Then start at the desk, but look around first. Make sure there are no security cameras."

They watched as her brother snapped a pair of latex gloves on and did a quick scan of the ceilings. No cameras. That didn't always mean anything, but they'd have to roll with it and hope Molly didn't have a camera hidden in a picture frame.

Joey located the cable outlet behind the credenza near Molly's desk. Dragging some tools out, he set them on the credenza, then turned back, checking the doorway.

Ro clucked her tongue. "Maybe I should go in there and distract the receptionist."

"No," Lucie said. "If we need to, I'll go in. We'll put our gassy friend back here to work."

"Man," Joey said, keeping his voice barely a whisper, "this chick is a neat freak. Luce, I thought you were bad." He slid open the second desk drawer where files were evenly spaced.

"Joey, look for a file with Reuben LeBeau's name on it. Be careful not to mess anything up. If she's like me, she'll notice if someone's been in her space."

"Nothing," Joey said. "This is all banking and tax stuff. Doesn't look like client files."

Leave it to them to find a paperless office when it came to client files.

"Do you see a filing cabinet?"

Joey looked around, his head moving so fast the image on screen bounced.

"No filing cabinet."

The sound of the receptionist's heels clicking sounded.

"Shit." Joey grabbed one of the tools from the top of the

credenza and hit the deck, once again sending the images on the iPad bouncing.

"Everything all right in here?"

"I'm good." He called from his spot on the floor. He sat up and faced the receptionist who stood in the doorway. "Do you mind if I move this credenza?"

Ah, nice touch.

He held up his gloved hands. "It's so neat in here, I didn't want to get fingerprints on anything."

Good one.

The receptionist smiled. "That's considerate. Move whatever you need to, as long as you put it back."

"Sure thing."

She took off again and Joey hopped to his feet, making the screen wobble again. Did he have to move so fast? If he kept that up, vertigo would set in.

He opened the credenza doors, found various office supplies, pens, stapler, tape, and the all-important pen cup. Yep, Molly liked things neat and tidy.

He rummaged through the two smaller cabinets, finding a stack of magazines and some scrapbooks with news clippings. He flipped through the scrapbooks.

"What's in there?"

"There's some stuff about Antoine. Articles. Guessing it's all clippings about clients."

He finished his perusal of the inside pages, then checked the back cover, running his fingers over the edges, no doubt looking for secret compartments. One thing about growing up a mob kid, you knew how to hide things. And if Molly and Reuben were in cahoots against Antoine, maybe Molly stashed the evidence.

"Nothing," he said. "I'll check the bookshelf."

He peered back at the doorway. Empty. On his way to the

bookshelf he halted, slowly turning his head to a large framed print on the wall.

"What?"

"The picture. When we were in high school, I always used to hide weed behind that framed poster in my room."

Lucie's mouth fell. Of all the crazy things Joey had ever said—and there were a lot—this one held the distinction of astonishing her. "You smoked *weed?* Joey!"

"Seriously?" Ro said. "You? A pothead?"

"Hey, it was high school. I got over it quick. I didn't like it. Dealing with you two? It might be an option again."

"Ha," Ro said. "Wise guy."

He peeped behind the frame.

"Nothing."

"Darn."

"Hang on. I'll check behind the bookcase."

Click, click, click. The receptionist again.

Joey glanced back at the doorway and the receptionist appeared. "Is everything all right?"

Ro grunted. "She's a pain in the year, this woman."

"Yeah," he said, cool as could be. Lucie wasn't sure who he was responding to. "I'm checking to see if there's another outlet behind this bookcase. I'm good."

The receptionist nodded and disappeared again.

Not good. Two visits didn't instill a sense of calm. Plus, the prickles shooting down Lucie's neck didn't help.

"Joey, she must be suspicious. You need to get out of there."

"Wha, wha. I'm right here. Let me check this real quick."

He slid a flashlight from his tool bag and shined it into the tiny space between the wall and bookcase.

Something caught Lucie's eye, but Joey moved and the image onscreen blurred.

"Wait," she said. "Look down again."

Joey tipped his head down, shining the flashlight as he went.

"There."

Taped to the back of the bookcase was a large manila envelope.

"Got it," he whispered. "It's an envelope."

Lucie and Ro stared at each other. What to do? If they didn't look, they'd never know.

"See if the envelope is sealed," Lucie said.

Joey gripped the bookcase, nudging it out enough to get his beefed-up arm behind it. "It's sealed," he said. "But it's one of those self-sticking ones. I think I can get it open without ripping it."

"Be careful."

He checked the doorway again, and Lucie's stomach flipped for non-Vertigo reasons. What were they doing invading this woman's privacy like this?

Whatever guilt plaguing her wasn't enough to stop the madness. Joey carefully pried the envelope open, wincing a little as the paper echoed in the quiet room.

Inside was an index card. A blue one that made Lucie's heart thump. He slid the card out giving Lucie and Ro a view of the front.

Cassoulet de Toulouse.

"Oh, wow," Lucie said. "That's it. That's the recipe."

The sudden urge to pee assailed Lucie. Damned flop-peeing. Her kidneys ballooned and she crossed her legs.

Had they just busted Molly blackmailing her own boyfriend? And client?

Lucie pressed her palm to her forehead. "We shouldn't get ahead of ourselves."

"Please," Ro said. "Why would she have a copy of that recipe pasted to her bookcase?"

"I don't know."

"Well, I'll tell you why. She needed a quick, temporary place to hide it while she puts the screws to her client. And I don't mean between the sheets either."

"Hey, you two," Joey's voice cut in. "Decision time. Am I taking this recipe or leaving it?"

From the driver's seat, Ro peered at Lucie. "I say take it. We can return it to Antoine, save him a few mil, and this whole thing will be over."

A nice plan if... Lucie shook her head. "We can't take it. How would we explain it? Even if we return it to Antoine, he'll think we chickened out of blackmailing him. He won't believe *Molly* stole it. According to him, she's a security freak and didn't want hard copies laying around."

"Tick-tock," Joey said.

Lucie went back to the iPad, where the camera recorded everything. "Leave it. If we take it, then we have no proof it was there."

"We'll have the video."

"Eh," Joey said. "Anyone with half a brain could explain that away. Maybe this card is a dupe. How do we know?"

Lucie rested her head back and stared out the windshield.

A very tall, very redheaded Irish detective marched to the entrance of Molly's office.

Panic sent Lucie rocketing forward, gripping the dashboard, and considering all the ways to put herself out of her own misery. Then again, she might not have to worry about that. *He'll kill us.*

Ro whipped her head around. "What?"

"It's Tim."

"O'Hottie? Where?"

"At the door. He's going in. Joey! Get out. Now. Tim is coming in."

"What now?"

"You heard me."

"What the hell, Luce? Why is your boyfriend here?"

As if she knew? "Oh, did I forget to mention I wanted him to catch us snooping in Molly's office?" She held up her fists and frustration poured into them. "How the hell should I know why he's there?"

The line went silent for a few seconds. "Joey?"

"Yeah. He's talking to the chick at the desk. Something about warning businesses about robberies in the area. Shit."

Lucie and Ro exchanged an *eek* look. "What?"

Lucie looked down at the iPad. Her brother swung his head side to side, once again making the image jump. "What are you doing?"

"He's coming back to use the john. I gotta hide."

On screen, he dropped to his knees behind Molly's desk. Lucie's kidneys sent up a warning flare.

"I have to pee so bad right now."

Ro handed her the soda cup from the console. "Dump the ice and have at it."

Ew. "I'm not doing that. I'll hold it."

Or not.

"Joey?"

"Shh."

She glanced down at the screen, at the wingtip dress shoes entering the frame. Joey raised his head, staring straight up.

At Tim.

"Dude," her brother said, "funny running into you here."

Tim stood over Joey, his blood pressure climbing thirty digits. By now, his hair might be standing on end.

For two days, he'd been cruising by this office, surveilling it when time allowed, and generally keeping an eye out for oddities when...hello...there was Joey.

Dressed in khakis and a golf shirt.

Talk about odd.

He checked over his shoulder before speaking. No nosey receptionist to be seen, but he'd keep this short and sweet anyway. He slapped on his best hardened-cop face. The one where his jaw nearly broke into chunks from the tension. "Joey. What. The. Fuck?"

Had to be one of Lucie's half-baked schemes.

"Yeah." Joey hopped to his feet. "This has gotta look bad."

Tim gave him the dead eyes. "Ya think?" He took in Joey's khaki pants, a first for sure. "What's with the getup? And since when do you wear glasses?"

"Uh, they're new. I'm trying them out. Been having headaches. Hang on a sec." Joey held his hand up and spoke into his wrist. "Shut it. Both of you."

The tension in Tim's jaw released as his mouth fell open. Joey having a two-way radio might just tip the insanity scale beyond its limit.

Tim pointed. "Is that Lucie? Seriously? You have a two-way radio?"

"It's both of them. They're making me nuts."

"Where the hell are they?"

Had to be close. Probably within eyesight of the front door. Tim turned, ready to hightail it out before Lucie and Ro got wise and made a break for it. *Crap...*

Receptionist in the doorway, peering at them with her big, nosey eyes. "Is everything all right?"

Tim nodded. "Yeah. All good. I saw him in here and decided to check him out." He pointed to Joey's *credentials*. "All good."

"Great. Thanks so much for doing that." The receptionist stepped back, sending the not-so-subtle hint that he should vacate the space they were in. Whoever's office this was—Tim assumed it to be Molly's—she wanted them out. Interesting.

She gestured to her left. "The bathroom is at the end of the hall."

If he wasted precious seconds making like he needed to use the bathroom, Lucie and Ro would be long gone. Running like hell from the lashing he'd give them for whatever this insane stunt was.

"Thanks. I just got a call though. Gotta run."

He stormed the hallway, his legs getting him to the door in record time. Once outside, he looked left, then panned right, his cop's eyes taking in every possible hiding place—trees, porches, parked cars.

There. Ro's Escalade parked in a fire zone. Yeah, that wasn't obvious at all.

Damn them.

He hit the sidewalk at a light jog and pointed. "Don't move!"

10

IPAD IN HAND, LUCIE FLINCHED. THE MOVEMENT SENT UP another cry from her engorged bladder.

Tim ran across the street, his big shoulders back in that commanding way she loved about him—so hot. But right now, her man's face was all mean cop.

We're so cooked.

Beside her, Ro gripped the wheel. "Here he comes. Duck!"

She threw herself sideways, slamming into Lucie. Their heads banged and the blast caused a flash of white spots to erupt.

"Ow," Lucie said. "What are you *doing*? He already sees us. Ducking won't help."

Lucie rubbed the side of her forehead, wincing at the contact. Darn it, that hurt.

Ro sat up, her face all scrunched with pain. She checked the rearview for any damage. "You have a major hard head."

That made two of them.

Knock, knock, knock.

The window.

Sonny poked his head through the bucket seats and let out a bark. Her protector. Refusing to look, Lucie kept her gaze fixed on Ro. "It's him, right?"

Dumb question. Who else would it be? Santa?

Ro peered beyond Lucie's shoulder and her lips froze into a petrified smile. "Oh, it's him. And he looks pissed."

Knock, knock, knock.

"Open up," Tim said.

"Luuuuucie," Ro said in her Ricky Ricardo accent, "we've got some 'splainin' to do."

Ro unlocked the doors and Tim hopped in the back. Sonny's tail whipped back and forth at the prospect of another human that might give him attention.

Joey strode out of the building and glanced their way. "Pick me up around the corner. That chick is squirrelly. She might be watching me."

"Roger that."

Again with the military verbiage? If Lucie wasn't about to wet herself, she might laugh. Might. Ro hit the gas, bolting into the roadway, cutting off a car cruising the street. A loud horn blast cracked the air. The violated driver stuck his hand out the window and flipped the bird.

Ro hit the window button and returned the gesture. "Go slap yourself."

"Roseanne," Tim said from the back seat, "try not to get us killed. Off, Sonny. You pain in the ass."

Lucie peeked back and found the dog climbing on Tim's lap trying to steal a lick or twelve. How adorable was he?

Dogs just knew how to break tension, and Lucie needed to tag team the effort. She met Tim's eye and felt her bladder wave that white flag again. Oh, the pressure. Still, she needed to focus on the situation. She held up one hand. "I know you're mad, but don't yell at him. He didn't do anything."

"Atta, girl, Luce," Ro said. At the corner, she hooked a right and pulled into the fire lane in front of the dry cleaners. "Dry cleaners," she said into her lip mic. "Get in on my side. O'Hottie is here and he's not pulling punches."

Lucie glanced down at the iPad and spotted her brother turning the corner right behind where they were parked. He whipped off the lanyard with his fake ID and shoved it into his jacket pocket.

After finally dealing with Sonny by scooping him up and petting him, Tim poked his head through the seats. "Who wants to tell me what the hell is going on?"

Best defense is a good offense. Lucie whipped around, poking a finger at him. "I could ask you the same thing. Why were *you* in Molly Jacardi's office?"

Tim made a buzzing noise. "Nice try. I've been cruising by that office a couple of times a day. Keeping an eye on things. And lucky thing or I wouldn't have spotted you lunatics. Doing whatever the hell it is you're doing."

The rear driver's side door opened and Joey hopped in. Sonny craned his neck and Joey eyeballed him.

"Don't do it, dog."

Sonny took the hint and burrowed further into Tim. Damned, Joey. How did he *do* that?

Rather than risk a ticket for parking in a fire zone, Ro hit the gas, once again bullying her way into traffic while Joey stowed his tool bag in the cargo area behind him.

Lucie glanced back, and found him pointing at Tim. "I don't wanna hear it," Joey said.

"You're gonna hear it. Do you know what that stunt could have cost you? And I'm not talking just a trespassing charge. Who the hell even knows if impersonating a cable guy is an offense? As long as I've been a cop, *that's* a new one. But hey, cable companies cross state lines. That's federal, my friend. And the recording? You didn't stop at video, you went full bore with audio. Guess what, kids? People are granted a reasonable expectation of privacy. You were in their office, recording without their knowledge. Any decent prosecutor could trump up a privacy violation on that."

Lucie let out an exaggerated sigh. "You're getting carried away. Joey was trying to *help* me."

"I get that. What I *don't* get is how three intelligent adults agreed on that half-assed stunt."

Lucie made eye contact with Joey. What could she possibly say? Between her brother dressed in his un-Joey getup, the stupid glasses, and Tim being a human lie detector, she had no fallback plan.

Tim set Sonny down, and the dog's head swung back and forth as if this was some grand adventure.

The tiny *pfft* of breaking wind sounded.

Joey cracked his window and shoved his face in the opening. "Man, this dog has wicked gas."

"He's a beast," Ro said. "The government should use him as an interrogating technique."

Lucie peeked back at Tim. His normally loving green eyes had turned...hard. His stiff posture and all that contained anger begging to burst free didn't help her straining bladder.

She'd made a disaster out of this situation. Her own fault for letting her family talk her into Joey searching Molly's office.

She couldn't blame them, though. Being a big girl meant taking ownership of her mistakes. Her miscalculations.

In her quest to make things right, she'd gone...cuckoo.

Now she needed to fix it. "I know you're mad."

"You sent your brother into that woman's office under a false identity, probably looking to steal something. Mad is reasonable."

"First of all, we didn't intend on *stealing* anything. We only wanted to peek at her files. Joey found the envelope with the recipe. *That* we didn't expect."

Tim's head snapped back, her revelation apparently draining his ire.

Dang. If she'd been thinking straight, she'd have led with the recipe and avoided getting her man all twisty. She'd been so busy formulating her defense, she hadn't realized Tim missed Joey discovering the envelope.

Clunking herself on the head, she faced front again as Ro circled the block, dodging traffic and filthy hand gestures.

"You missed that part," Lucie said. "Joey found an envelope with a copy of Antoine's recipe in it. On a blue index card."

"No way."

"Yes way."

Tim rested his elbow on the doorframe and rubbed his forehead.

"Headache?"

He laughed.

Of course he had a headache. Dealing with them? What did she expect?

"This envelope? Where was it?"

Joey took that one. "Taped to the back of the bookcase."

"And that was Molly's office?"

Lucie nodded. "Yes. You were there when Antoine told us Molly is a security freak and didn't want him keeping hard copies of the recipe around. If that's true, why is there a copy hidden behind her bookshelf?"

Tim held his finger up. "Is she a control freak?"

Ro let out a snort and made another right turn. "O'Hottie, I think you are losing your mind. What does it matter if she's a control freak?"

"Maybe she doesn't like him being subversive by keeping a hard copy in his safe and she's teaching him a lesson. I've seen nuttier things."

"Huh," Ro said, suddenly not so skeptical.

Ro took the next turn a little sharper than necessary and Lucie jerked sideways, nearly getting decapitated by the seatbelt. Rather than suffer an injury, she faced front, noodling the control freak theory.

"Maybe she wants to teach Antoine a lesson, so she took the recipe."

Joey leaned in. "But taking it isn't enough. She's ballsy, this one. She's gonna put the screws to him. Keep him in his place and prove she's right."

"By stealing his recipe and then pretending to be a blackmailer?" Ro shook her head. "Not buying it."

Lucie bit her lip. "Why?"

"It's too risky. What if he called the cops?"

"She knew he wouldn't," Tim said. "They're a couple. She knows his hot buttons. He made it damned clear he didn't want this to get out. She'd know that about him. Hell, if she's the security nut, she might have conditioned him to be this way."

On the fourth pass around the block, Tim backhanded the edge of Ro's seat. "Pull over on that corner. Let me out."

He was still mad. Lucie sensed it. Not so much by his words or his body language, but the lack of all that. The neutrality. When it came to work, to investigating cases, Tim's poker face could win him millions in Vegas.

But this wasn't work. Not totally. This was about her—and him—and generally he kicked the poker face to the curb when it came to her.

She turned back again, but he stared out the window, his mind clearly moving to the next task.

"You're leaving?" Lucie asked.

After a long minute, he met her gaze. Those pretty green eyes weren't nearly as frigid as they had been a few minutes ago, but they didn't exactly scream friendly either.

Still mad.

"Luce, I'm in the middle of my workday. I'll look into this. See what I can dig up on Molly Jacardi. But, please, give me a friggin' break. No more screwball schemes."

"Well," Ro said, "that was fun."

Lucie stared out the window at pedestrians huddled into their coats, hands tucked in pockets, fighting the cold. Not Tim though. He strode to his car completely ignoring the weather. Of course, he had enough steam to keep him warm. "He was really mad."

"Eh," Ro waved it off. "He'll get over it."

In Ro and Joey's world, yelling and knockdown arguments occurred on a daily basis. If they weren't mad at each other, something was wrong. They were twisted that way. Tim? Not his style. Anger, for him, sucked too much energy. Energy he needed to get through the depravity he saw in his day job.

Lucie rested her elbow on the door and her chin in her hand. "Tim doesn't get mad a lot."

"Crap," Joey said from the backseat. "This field trip put me behind schedule. Ro, do me a favor, drop me off at the Lutzes'. I'll get Otis walked now and it'll save me time."

Otis? Lucie perked up. After this fiasco, a little Otis love might be just the thing Lucie needed to clear her mind. To regroup.

"I'll go with you. Seeing the big lug always clears my head. Stop at that donut shop around the corner so I can pee. I'm dying."

Twenty minutes later, Ro slipped into another fire zone near Otis's house. Lucie and Joey hopped out.

"I'll stay here," Ro said. She shifted to park and retrieved a nail file from the center console. "Don't be long. We have work to do back at the office."

Never mind the fire zone.

Lucie and Joey tromped up the driveway and entered the garage door code. The Lutzes, given the cushy neighborhood and the bankroll they'd dropped on the teardown and new construction of their home, had the luxury of a garage. The door silently opened. Not a creak or a squeak to be heard. Noise wouldn't dare.

Mrs. L's car sat in its normal spot. She was home. Good. With her husband—Lucie's former boss—doing a short prison stint for fraud, Mrs. L had gone to work part-time. Not so much for the money, but to occupy time. Watching her own mother grapple with the humiliation of a jailbird husband, Lucie understood the initial panic and stifling fear over how to support a household. Throw in the loneliness and Lucie never wanted to experience any of it.

Lucie and Joey approached the inside garage entry, and Otis let out a woof.

"Hey, buddy," Lucie called in her *I'm-so-excited* voice before Joey even had the door open.

Otis woofed again. A few seconds later a loud thump came from the other side of the door.

"Don't jump," Lucie scolded.

The big guy, an Olde English Bulldogge, had to be eighty-five pounds by now. All that weight flying against Mrs. L's door couldn't be good.

"See," her brother said, "this is why you're a disaster as a dog walker. Why would you get him so wound up before I even have the damned door open?"

He turned the handle, but the door wouldn't budge.

Joey grunted. "Great. He's blocking the door."

Her mountain of a brother threw his formidable weight into the door, pushing it open.

Otis's giant head poked into the opening. His toothy under bite gave him a bad-to-the-bone appearance, but this dog was hardly a menace to society. Total mush.

After Joey's scolding, she contained her enthusiasm, but bent over and nuzzled his snout. "Hi, sweet boy. I missed you."

Otis offered up a lick or two then moved on to Joey, who squatted and gave him a good rub. "What's up, dude? You ready for your walk?"

"Well, hello, you two."

Lucie glanced up to where Mrs. L stood in the kitchen doorway. She wore skin-tight jeans, black leather boots, and a silk blouse. The ensemble screamed casual, but somehow Mrs. L always embodied elegance. The boots alone could probably pay someone's mortgage.

Lucie waved. "Hi. I'm crashing. Was in the neighborhood and figured I'd come and see my boy. I miss the bugger."

"You know he loves you. How've you been?"

"I'm good. Busy."

Grabbing the leash from the hook, Joey clipped it on. "I'm gonna get him started. You can catch up, Luce."

Huh. Look at him, worrying about staying on time. And he teased her about her scheduling obsession?

"Okay. Thanks." She closed the door behind Joey and faced Mrs. L. "How's everything here? How is Mr. L?"

Lucie's emotions regarding her former boss were still in flux. She'd always appreciate what he'd done for her career wise, but he'd also betrayed her. She'd trusted him, and he allowed her to get caught up in a financial fraud scheme that could have landed her in jail. Right next to him.

"He's fine. I visited over the weekend. He asks about you all the time. He feels terrible about what he did to you."

As well he should. "Send him a hello for me. I'm not holding any grudges." Not many, anyway. "When he comes home, we'll talk."

"He'd like that."

Being a girl who'd rather pass on negativity, she'd forgiven him. More for herself than him. She simply didn't need to carry the anger and hurt around each day.

Didn't mean she'd trust him again.

Ever.

He'd been her mentor, the one who gave her a chance as a summer associate and had enough faith in her to hire her straight out of grad school. He'd taught her the ins and outs of investment banking. How to navigate the treacherous waters of deal-making and not piss off the banking regulators. For that, she'd be grateful.

Wait.

Regulators. Mr. L's contacts. Major contacts. Ones who might be able to tell her if Molly Jacardi had a history of shady dealings. It wouldn't prove she was currently blackmailing her client, but it would reveal her character. Or lack thereof.

Lucie paused, staring at Mrs. L in her silk blouse and diamond earrings while her mind zipped.

"Lucie?"

He owes me.

Lucie clunked herself on the head. "Sorry. My mind drifted. Mrs. L, could I ask a favor?"

"Of course."

"I know you and Mr. L have a lot of friends in finance. I'm in the middle of a...deal...right now. An...expansion of sorts."

"Good for you, Lucie. That's lovely."

Hardly. "We'll see. I've made a contact that I'd like to check on." Lucie waved a hand. "You know, just to make sure they don't have any financial violations out there."

"Oh, sure." Mrs. L pursed her lips. "Our friend Milt works for FinCEN. I could put a call in for you if you'd like."

The Financial Crimes Enforcement Network. As a bureau of the Treasury Department, it was FinCEN's job to monitor the financial system for illegal transactions.

"Since you're here," Mrs. L said, "let's do it right now."

Perfect. "Thank you. That would be great."

———

MR. L's FRIEND MILT WAS IN A MEETING, SO LUCIE SENT RO and Joey home and killed time with Mrs. L while waiting. With the day slipping and no returned call, she finally hauled herself back to the office.

Ro sat at her desk, pencil tucked behind her ear as she stared at a sketch pad. The cover had been thrown over

Felix's cage, indicating their ever-chatty parrot had pushed Ro's nerves to their limits.

"Don't fucking do it!" Felix squawked from underneath his sheath.

Ro slammed her palm against the desk. "That bird is lucky I haven't put him on a spit."

"He doesn't like the cover."

"Then he should shut up and learn. The only time I put the cover on is when he annoys me with that damned squawking. And don't start about how he got me out of prison. I'm *well* aware. But there's only so much I can take."

Drama, drama, drama.

Lucie pulled the cover off, and Felix swung his head back and forth. "I know, pal. Are you hungry?"

"Yes," Felix said.

Ro let out a dramatic sigh. "He's totally playing you."

Probably. "Let's try feeding him. That usually quiets him down."

Just as Lucie finished dealing with Felix, her cell phone rang. A DC number.

The FinCEN guy. *Goodie.*

"This is Lucie."

"Lucie, hello. This is Milt Savage returning your call."

Milt Savage. What a freaking awesome name. "Hello. Thank you for calling back."

"Sure. The Lutzes are good friends. What can I do for you?"

"I'm assuming you talked to Mrs. L?"

Ro shot Lucie a look, squinting a bit as she tried to figure out who was on the phone.

"I did," Milt said. "She said you needed help regarding a new business venture."

"Yes. I worked for Mr. Lutz as his assistant for a couple of years. I have my own business now and am considering partnering with someone. That person is represented by a manager, who I'm assuming will be handling the contracts and money for her client."

A brief hesitation filled the phone line. Friendship or not, this man was a government employee. Sharing personal information about citizens wasn't just unethical, it was illegal.

"I see," he said.

Yep. Totally losing him. "Obviously, I come from the finance world. I understand the ramifications of sharing information. I don't expect that. I simply want to make sure I know who I'm getting into business with."

"Understandable."

"I know you are limited as to what you can tell me."

Now Ro's eyebrows went up and she waved her hands. "Who's that? Put it on speaker so I can hear."

As if.

"I am, indeed," Milt said.

This didn't sound hopeful and—*wow*—suddenly Lucie seemed pretty darned assertive, asking this man to risk so much for a stranger. What the heck was she doing?

Guilt slammed her and she closed her eyes. *Dope.* Her single-minded effort to clear her name had seriously botched her thinking.

"You know what," she said. "Never mind. This was a bad idea. I'm so sorry to put you in this position."

"Lucie?"

"Yes?"

"Can I call you right back?"

Huh? Maybe he had another call? "Of course."

She disconnected. Ro, apparently done keeping her curiosity at bay, held her hands out. "What's that about?"

Lucie pointed to the phone. "Milt Savage. He's a friend of Mr. Lutz."

"The rat-bastard."

"The rat-bastard with contacts at the Treasury Department and the Financial Crimes Network."

"Ooh, nice."

"Exactly. He's checking Molly out for me. If there's any suspicious activity on Molly's accounts, I can have Tim look into it. He's law enforcement. They can get banks to pony up information."

Ro waggled one of her red-tipped fingers. "You know what the whole calling you back thing means, right?"

"Um, maybe he got another call?"

"*Pfft*. Are you kidding? He's afraid his work phone is monitored. He's calling back on a secure line. *So* James Bond."

Lucie's phone rang and she checked the number. A different one this time.

"It's a new number, isn't it?"

"Yes, but—"

"Ha! Knew it."

"Hello?"

"Lucie? Milt Savage again. Sorry. I didn't want to talk on my office line."

Well, holy moly. The drama queen was right.

"Told ya," Ro said, heavy on the smug.

Lucie stuck her tongue out. "That's fine," she said to Milt. "But really, I don't want to put you in a bad position. I realize I'm asking a lot here."

"You haven't asked me anything yet. What is it that you want me to do?"

Maybe this wasn't such a bust after all. "I was hoping you might be able to tell me, without specifics, if there have been any suspicious activity reports filed on someone."

Another long pause ensued. This guy didn't even know her. The banking world could be treacherous, though, and plenty of the players made side deals or shared information.

Right now, all she needed was a yes or no. Perhaps, given her relationship with the Lutzes, he'd trust her enough to provide it.

"Give me the name."

A burst of adrenaline spurted into Lucie's system and she swung her free hand in the air. *Yay, me.* "You'll do it?"

"Lucie, I worked for Daniel Lutz myself. He made a mistake, but he gave me a career. For him, I'll do this. I'll give you a yes or no on the SARs, but that's it."

"Thank you. Believe me, I know what I'm asking. If it weren't important, I wouldn't. And I promise to keep this between us. The name is Molly Jacardi."

"I'll call you back."

Lucie punched off and set her phone on the desk, spinning it around.

Ro shook her head. "Luce, what are you doing?"

"What?"

"Don't even. Didn't O'Hottie just tell you to stay out of it?"

Lucie held up a finger. "He said no more schemes. He didn't say anything about research."

Semantics. Sometimes they saved the day. Or Lucie's behind when Tim got hold of her.

Ro peeped at her over the funky reading glasses Lucie wasn't all that sure she actually needed.

"Now you're dreaming. He's not even *my* boyfriend and I'm sure he meant no activity on this at all. Period. Zip-*oh*."

Well, too bad. Certain things she'd risk. Lucie stabbed

her finger into the desktop. "The ransom drop is tomorrow. If Antoine gives the blackmailer that money, it'll disappear and he'll still think I'm the one who stole his recipe. I can't have that. Tim doesn't understand. It's easy for him to say stay out of it. It's not his reputation on the line."

"Honey, you don't have to preach to me. I know you better than anyone. If going against O'Hottie gets you where you need to be, I'm right there with you. Always. You know that."

This was friendship. Bury-the-body or, more appropriately, bury-the-secret friendship. Lucie held her breath a second, reminded herself that, despite her current predicament, most people didn't have Ro—as wacky as she was—and the love that came with her.

"I know you are," Lucie said. "I love Tim, but he hasn't lived this life with me. You have."

"You know it, sister. As crazy as I think you are, I see where you're going with this. If you prove Molly is crooked, it helps your theory on her blackmailing her boo thang."

"Thank you. See, this is critical information to have."

"Yeah, but His Hotness will still kill you."

11

A little after seven o'clock that night, Lucie stood on Tim's front porch wondering whether to ring the bell or just use her key.

Any other time she'd avoid standing in the cold and make no bones about walking right in. They were in love after all.

Except, after the unrelated-to-the-weather chill factor that afternoon, she didn't want to assume anything. Tim might not even want her there. Something she'd avoided confirming by failing to call and alert him of her visit.

Why take that chance when she could just pop over, apologize for inducing near fatal blood pressure spikes, and hopefully—*eh-hem*—make it up to him?

She'd learned the hard way that when dealing with Tim and apologies, sex wasn't a bad option.

This was what her life had come to. Emotional prostitution.

Eh, there were worse things.

She hit the buzzer and shoved her hands into her coat pockets while she waited. Thirty seconds in, Tim opened the door. He wore basketball shorts and a tank top that showed off his beefed-up biceps.

His eyebrows hitched. "Why didn't you use your key?"

"You didn't know I was coming. I thought…" Ooh, how to put this without making him mad again? She shrugged. "I thought you might still be mad at me."

"And what? That means you can't use your key?" He stepped back. "Get in here. And unless I tell you it's not okay to use your key, use your key."

"Thank you."

"You have to stop doing that."

A noise came from the second-floor landing. His nosey neighbor liked to open his door and listen in on conversations happening in the common area.

Tim jerked his head. "Let's go inside."

She followed him into his apartment and slid off her coat, laying it over the arm of the well-loved sofa his brother had given him. "What do I have to stop doing?"

He faced her, crossing his arms. All she really wanted was for him to put those arms around her. *Not this time.*

"If I'm mad, it doesn't mean I never want to see you again. Last I checked, we were in a relationship. People fight, Luce."

He was telling *her* that? With the crew she ran with? "I know. Of course I do. But our situation is different. Don't you think?"

"Because I'm a cop and you're Joe Rizzo's daughter."

Uh…yeah. "It makes me nervous. I love you and I never— ever— want you to suffer for that."

"If you haven't noticed, every time you try to protect me, you make it worse."

Ouch. Had he really just said that? She squeezed her eyes closed and pondered the fact that men must have been born idiots. It was in their DNA. They couldn't help it.

Still, over the last few months, troubles plagued her. In each instance, she'd tried to avoid involving Tim. And forcing him to compromise his integrity. He should at least recognize that.

"Give me credit for trying."

He cupped her cheeks with his big hands—finally—and the warmth of his palms penetrated her cold skin. "I do. Believe me. I *know* who you are. Kinda hard to miss that in this town. Luce, I went into this with my eyes wide open."

"But, in the beginning—"

"Yeah. In the beginning I didn't advertise who my girlfriend was. We agreed on that. Now? My boss knows. It's out there. I'm not hiding it. These damned investigations of yours are killing me, though. When you go behind my back, I can't help you and then I'm blindsided. *That's* what puts me in a bad spot. Not your last name."

Okay, but...what? When he made it sound so...logical... how was she supposed to respond? She gripped his wrists and held on, loving the way his skin felt under her hands. And it hit her, the want, the sudden desperation. With Frankie, she'd loved him, but this? This neediness? She'd never allowed that.

Not until now. "I just..." She closed her eyes a second, focused on choosing the right words.

"What?"

She opened her eyes and met his gaze, holding it for a long few seconds. "I don't want to get you in trouble. That's all."

His mouth quirked and he shook his head before pressing a kiss to her forehead. "Honey, I'm a big boy. I don't need you making decisions for me."

Tim was done.

Done having this conversation and done with Lucie not trusting his intentions. He loved this girl, and she couldn't get past her fear that he'd dump her.

Because of her last name.

So either he'd done a piss-poor job of proving it didn't matter or she didn't want to believe it. Either way, it had to stop.

Screwball investigations or not, he wanted her in his life. These last few months he'd been trying to mold Joe Rizzo's daughter into his life. The life of a law enforcement officer.

How's that working?

Not so good.

What he needed was to forget about Joe Rizzo's daughter and think about Lucie. Sweet, lovable Lucie, who never quit. On anything. That's who he wanted. Not the so-called mob princess. He'd been balancing on the wire between his cop world and her mob world. Wasn't that the thing she'd been running from her entire adult life? People treating her a certain way based on her lineage?

Son of a bitch.

However evolved he considered himself, he'd done the exact thing she'd been complaining about. And he'd been on her about her investigations. Constantly telling her to stop, which, yeah, he wanted her to do. But was it fair? Wanting everything his way? No compromises.

That needed to change.

He met her gaze, that deep, haunting blue that gave him a hitch in his chest every time. "I love you. Period. All this time, I've been trying to balance it all. You on one side, my job on the other. And I've been hassling you."

"You haven't been—"

He held up a hand. "Fine. But I haven't been agreeable. All of it snowballed. You don't want to involve me. Meanwhile, I'm trying to protect you and you're keeping secrets to protect me. Damned vicious cycle."

He'd just never realized it until now. All this time, he'd been managing situations, handling them as best he could. His way.

He shook his head. "I'm done trying to scare you into not doing your screwball investigations. Today, that stops. I'd still prefer you not investigate, but I hate the secrets and I hate that I put you in a position to keep them. It's you and me. Tim and Lucie. No Joe Rizzo's kid. No cop. Just us. Together. Okay?"

Tears welled up in her eyes and that stupid hitch in his chest became a tight ball. *Damn.* Lucie crying might be the worst thing he'd ever seen.

She bobbed her head. "Tim and Lucie. I'd love that."

"I mean, I could do without the screwy investigations, but..."

She laughed. "Me too! I hate them. I just get sucked in and...you know me, I can't let go."

"I do know. It's the thing I love most about you. Which, hello? Also makes me insane. You always fight. No matter what. My girl never gives up."

"It's in the DNA. Whether it was right or not, Dad taught me the art of battle."

Tim shrugged. "It's not a bad lesson."

"I'm learning that."

"Good."

He stepped closer, close enough to feel her breath on his face when he dipped his head to kiss her. As usual, she welcomed it, sliding her arms around his waist and bowing into him.

Tim and Lucie.

Lucie and Tim.

A fresh start. Zero baggage.

LUCIE FOUGHT THE EMOTION CLOGGING HER THROAT. TIM, THE man she'd spent the last months parceling information about her investigations to, had just spilled his guts. Had basically taken the blame for all the tension-filled moments between them.

Adoring him was so, so easy.

She couldn't blame him for how he felt about her investigations. They were adults, each with their own hang-ups and concerns. And there were worse things than a man who wanted to protect her. Now, it seemed, he wanted to find the compromise, the middle ground between completely stifling her and helping her.

The least she could do is be honest with him. As honest as he'd been with her.

I can do this.

She drew a long breath, held it for a second, and exhaled. She looked up at him, big, strong Tim O'Brien. *He can handle it.* "Full disclosure is about to happen. And remember what you just said."

"Ah, crap."

"Listen, Detective—"

Before she got too far into her defense, he pressed his index finger against her mouth. "No. I'm sorry. I shouldn't have said that. Old habits." He shook his head. "We're not arguing. It's us. Lucie and Tim. Give it to me straight."

Oh, boy. He asked for it. "After you left us today, I went with Joey to walk Otis. While we were there, I saw Mrs. Lutz and I thought about all the contacts Mr. L has."

"Okay."

"And, you know, he kinda owes me a favor, given the whole almost making me someone's prison bitch." Tim closed his eyes, clearly battling for patience. He rolled one hand and she nodded. "Right. So...I asked Mrs. Lutz if they knew anyone who could check Molly's finances. Nothing too intense. Just top-line stuff so we could figure out if she's done anything suspect."

Tim's mouth twisted. "I can live with that."

"Really?"

He shrugged. "I'd have done it. Did you break any laws?"

She took a few seconds with that one. "Eh, borderline."

Tim closed his eyes, the battle really raging now. "What did you do?"

"Mrs. L put me in touch with a friend who works at FinCEN. I asked him to check if there'd been any reports filed on Molly. Basic stuff. Cheating on her taxes, moving large sums of money, things like that."

"And?"

"Nothing. Clean as a whistle."

"*Really?*"

"Yep. He called me right before I got here. There haven't been any reports filed."

"Doesn't always mean anything. She could be good at hiding."

"I agree. I have an idea though."

One strawberry blond eyebrow lifted. God bless him, Tim was trying. She set her hands on his cheeks, went up on tiptoes, and kissed him quick, before he lost it on her. "I love this new openness. I feel like we've had a major breakthrough. I've hated hiding things from you, the one person who's always so steady and filled with good advice. This makes life so much easier."

"I'm glad you're happy." He twisted his mouth in a lame attempt to hide a smile. "It's killing me. But tell me your idea."

She squeezed his cheeks. "Dean."

"The hacker?"

"Yes. I think we should call him and ask him to snoop in Molly's email. That might tell us something. Particularly about her relationship with Reuben. Honestly though, I'm not feeling it on Reuben. He doesn't seem like a scummy blackmailer to me."

"And Molly does?"

"Good point."

Tim considered the suggestion, tipping his head one way then the other. Prior to the conversation they'd just had, she'd have hesitated to even bring it up. Now, with this new sense of open communication, she felt a freeing lightness, the weight of all those secrets lifted from her.

"Okay," Tim said.

Whoa. Did he just agree? "Fine, as in have Dean snoop?"

"Yeah. We've got nothing to lose. We're spying on everyone else. And the money drop is tomorrow morning. We're running out of time."

"Yes, we are." And speaking of the money... "We should plan on being at the drop. If the money disappears," she slashed her hand across her throat, "I'm cooked."

This suggestion might be pushing the boundaries of love, but what the heck. He wanted total honesty.

He crossed his arms, stared down at the floor a second. "A sting op."

At best, a vague statement. Still, it wasn't a no. Definitely history making strides in the Tim and Lucie relationship. Might as well push a little more, see how far O'Hottie would let this go. "I'm not familiar with that park, but we can get some dogs and walk them. We'll plant people all around and wait until the money is picked up. Then we follow it."

If he bought this idea, she'd know, without a doubt, he meant every word he'd said to her. Tim taking an active role in one of her formerly screwball ideas was monumental. Total dedication right there. A commitment.

Almost an engagement ring.

In her mind anyway.

Blame it on all the talk about a double wedding and the I-love-yous. What was a woman her age, with dreams of a family, supposed to think?

Lucia Rizzo O'Brien.

She rolled it around in her mind, let it settle. Something warm and fluttery stirred inside.

Wow. That felt...good.

Perfect, even.

Tim checked his watch. "The drop is set for 11:00 tomorrow. I'll take a sick day and run out to the park in the morning, get the lay of it. Then I'll meet you at your office. Can you get everyone together? Say 8:30 or 9:00. That'll give me time to work up a strategy."

Lucie nodded. "I can do that. Easy. I'll call them tonight."

Tim smacked his hands together. "Done deal. How about a quickie?"

Unbelievable.

"My endorphins are going," he said. "Made me horny. It's not uncommon."

Ro was right. Men were total rutting pigs.

But, darn, she loved them. This one in particular.

She nestled into him, wrapping her arms around his

waist, loving the feel of his tank top and that clean soapy smell. Tim and Lucie. Lucie and Tim.

Together.

She tipped her head up. "Maybe I want more than a quickie, Detective."

He kissed her with a soft brush of his lips. "I won't complain. Not when it comes to you. I love you. I want you always."

"Me too. I was just thinking about that."

"Maybe we should start talking about the future."

"Are you ready for that?"

"Honey, I'm thirty-five years old. I'm not getting any younger. I want a family and I don't plan on using a walker to coach my kids in sports."

She envisioned Tim on a basketball court, shouting instructions and patting a kid on the head. She liked it. The idea of them as parents, her popping out babies. Redheaded babies.

She curled into him again and held tight. "Let's talk about it. Not now, though. Tonight, I just want you."

Lucie held on, loving the feel of being so close. His big body wrapping around her much smaller one. She went up on tiptoes and kissed him. The kiss intensified and he slid his tongue inside her mouth and—*yay, me*—her body responded. Nothing new there. Every time Tim came near, her clothes begged to be discarded.

Tonight was no different.

She slid her hands down to the waistband of his shorts and tucked her thumbs inside.

Tim backed away an inch and smiled. "Slut."

"I know. It's horrible."

"I'll never complain."

"Good. Me neither." She leaned in, tipping her head

forward and resting it against his chest. Which gave her a perfect view of his growing erection. She brought one hand down and gave him a squeeze right through his shorts. Such. A. Slut. "Hello, mister."

"I've missed you, Luce."

She looked up, found his eyes on her in that hungry, feral way that made her feel loved and wanted. Beautiful, even.

And that was a gift.

"I love you," she said.

"I love *you*."

"Good. Now take me to bed and bang my lights out."

Tim let out a laugh, one of his good belly laughs that made his face light up. Who said she sucked at seduction? This boy was putty in her hands? Well, given the state of his groin area, putty might not have been a totally accurate description.

Go, Lucie.

He hoisted her up over his shoulder, smacking her on the ass as he headed to the bedroom.

"Let's do this," he said. "Then we've got a blackmailer to catch."

LUCIE'S OPERATIVES, ALL BRIGHT-EYED AND READY FOR action, began gathering at Coco Barknell at 8:30 AM sharp.

Undeterred by the chatter, Ro sat at her desk answering emails while Joey dealt with Dad's latest phone mishap. The two of them huddled up at the conference table, Dad in his usual dress slacks and shirt, his salt-and-pepper hair gelled into place. In contrast, Joey wore jeans and a long-sleeved T-shirt, his dark hair dipping below his ears and curling. Lucie took comfort in that. The normalcy of her brother and father. So alike, yet so different.

Joey poked around on Dad's phone. "You must have hit the camera. Or did you attach the picture?"

Dad shrugged. "You're asking me?"

Joey laughed. "Forget it. No harm done. It's not like you sent naked pictures of yourself to Aunt Doris."

Lucie gagged. Total nightmare.

Jimmy Two-Toes pushed through the shop door with Sonny trailing behind. Something outside grabbed the Jack Russell's attention—or maybe it was just a thirty-eight-degree sunny day a dog could enjoy.

"No. Come with Daddy."

Daddy?

Ro glanced over at her and bit her lip. Hey, even mob guys had soft spots.

Jimmy shook his head. "He hates being inside. Luce, you got any more of that food you gave him? It's got crack in it or something. He refuses to eat anything else now."

Impressive that. Considering Jimmy fed the dog rib-eye steaks.

"I don't. I'll see what I can do, though." Lucie squatted to give Sonny some almost-world-famous Lucie love. She snuggled him, scratching behind his ears in that spot he liked. "You liked that food, didn't you, boy?"

The doggie bells on the door jangled again. Mom and her friend Bev entered.

Mom tugged on the fingers of her gloves and whipped them off. "We're here to help. All hands on deck."

Excellent. Because if Lucie knew this crew at all, Ro would insist on coming and that would leave the shop unattended. With Mom here, she and Bev could handle the phones.

Mom pointed at Joey. "And before anyone says a word, Bev will handle the phones. I'm coming. I never get to do the fun stuff."

"No," Dad said.

Mom eyed him. "Listen, man-on-parole, I'm going. I don't care what you say."

Joey's mouth flopped open. Literally nosedived.

Go, Mom. A few years ago, if Dad had given an order like that, she'd have fallen right in line. Just sucked it up like a dutiful, obedient wife. No going against the man of the house and all that nonsense. Once Dad went away, Mom discovered independence had its perks. Big ones.

Like not being told what to do by men in prison.

Bent on female unity, Lucie grabbed a folder off her desk and headed to the conference table. "I like that idea, Mom. You and Dad can be a strolling couple."

Tim entered the shop, sending the doggie bells jangling again, and Lucie's skin heated up. Ooh-eee, what a night they'd had. But she shouldn't even be *thinking* about that in front of Dad.

"Morning," Tim said to the room at large.

"Hey, handsome." He set a duffle bag on the table and Lucie eyed it. "What's that?"

"Radios. I borrowed them from a buddy. There's six in there. The earpieces have a thin wire that hooks around your ear. Barely detectable."

"Cool," Joey said.

"We'll need them. I went to the park this morning. The area where the drop takes place is big. Wide open. We'll split the radios up so we can stay in constant contact."

Joey reached for the bag, ready to begin playing.

"Joseph," Mom said, sliding into the chair across from Dad, "remember how you loved walkie-talkies when you were little? You were so cute, climbing into the attic and talking to me. I miss those days."

Mom let out a little sigh and a small chunk of Lucie's heart broke free. It had to be hard. Being on the back half of life, children grown and building their own lives. Well, mostly.

Living alone with Dad.

Lawdy.

Taking care with the radios, Joey emptied the bag and lined the contents on the table.

"I'll show you how to use them," Tim said. "First, let's talk strategy."

"Ooh, fun," Mom said to Bev. "I'm sorry you're going to miss this."

"It's all right. I'm too old to be traipsing in the cold anyway. My arthritis is killing me."

Ro finally gave up on her emails and wandered over, her high-heels—the *walking* shoes—clicking against the tile. She took the open spot next to Joey.

Lucie nabbed the chair next to Mom, leaving the end spot for Tim, sending the clear message that the good detective was in charge. She flipped her folder open and distributed maps of the park she'd printed the night before.

"This is Cliffside park," Tim said, "It's five acres, but we're only concerned with this corner." He circled an area on the map and held it up for everyone to see. "We're watching for the money drop. Keep your eyes peeled. Radio me if there's anything suspicious. Anything that looks...off. I need to know. Antoine's been instructed to leave the money in a hollowed-out tree." Tim pointed at the spot on the map. "The tree is here. I saw it this morning. Once the exchange is made, I'll tail the person who picks up the bag."

Mom's lips dipped to a frown. "*That's* it? I put makeup on for this?"

Holding on to a laugh, Lucie took that one. "We're trying to identify suspects. Once we know who they are, we can prove I didn't steal the recipe. We'll show our proof to Antoine, then he'll decide what he wants to do." She grinned. "In addition to dropping that damned lawsuit."

Dad held up a finger. "Who are the suspects?"

"We think we've narrowed it to Molly," Lucie said. "Antoine's manager. And perhaps his friend Reuben. We're hoping today will tell us for sure."

She and Tim had discussed this at length last evening. Tim, being a cop, wanted to bring law enforcement in. To which Lucie countered that Antoine was the actual victim, and he'd chosen not to involve the police. He wanted to keep this quiet. Lucie couldn't blame him.

And, once Lucie proved her innocence, she still hoped to do an investment deal with Antoine. Outing him right now, after he'd made it clear he didn't intend on calling the police, wouldn't help her.

"I'd go another way," Dad said.

This should be good. Lucie took a long pull of air. "I'm sure you would."

"My way is better. Jimmy and me, we'll take care of this one, two, three."

Jimmy's head bobbed. "You and me, Joe. We got this."

Tim cleared his throat. Poor guy. A good honest cop surrounded by a mob boss, his cronie, and a dog named Sonny Corleone.

"No," Lucie said. "We're doing this legit."

"Assignments," Tim said, attempting to refocus the group. "Joey, you take the northeast section."

"Otis is coming with. I'm not looking like some kind of perv hanging around a park by myself. That's just wrong."

Now he wanted to bring Otis into this? Lucie held her hands out. "Did you clear that with Mrs. L?"

She'd redone the entire schedule last night to free up Joey and he intended on blowing the entire thing up.

"Yeah. I'm not looking like no perv."

Lucie whipped her cell phone out. "I'll let Lauren know she can skip Otis."

"Already done," Joey said.

Really?

"Don't look so shocked," Ro said. "He's good at this. You're just too type A to appreciate it. For a normal person, Joey's a rock star. You're a freak. Nothing compares."

Probably true.

"Thank you, Joey."

"No prob."

Ro waggled her hand, sending her bangle bracelets jangling. "Give me a good assignment. Something that doesn't require me half-naked."

Tim studied the map, an aerial view of the park Lucie had printed from the internet. He tapped the western edge of the section he'd circled. "Let's put you here. By this fountain."

"That works," Lucie said. "I lined up Boots for you. He's small, so he'll be easy to handle."

"I'll be fine. I have my walking shoes on."

At that, Tim snorted.

"We'll give Mom and Dad the Ninja Bitches."

"Oh," Mom said. "I love those two. So sassy."

Apparently, Dad wasn't feeling it. "Come on," he said, "you're giving me a couple of pansies?"

How offensive! Everyone always underestimated petite people. And dogs. "Dad," Lucie said, "don't mess with those girls. They'll take your leg off."

Clearly a non-believer, Dad gave her a thumbs-down. "They don't look like it. Give me the bull dog."

"No," Joey said. "He's mine. I love that dog."

Dad let out a huff. "Jesus Christmas, how embarrassing. I hope no one recognizes me."

"Assignments," Tim said, this time way louder than necessary. "Jimmy, you and Sonny are at the bottom here."

Lucie nodded. "That works. Then we have Mom and Dad strolling, Ro on the western edge, and Joey covering the east. You and I can sit somewhere and watch."

Tim studied the map, his lips moving one way then the

other. "That'll work. Luce, we'll get there early. Scope out a spot."

Lucie stepped away, retrieving the plastic grocery bag she'd tossed on her desk. "I brought my wig. Just in case Antoine spots me."

She and that blond wig had seen a lot of action together. Some of it in the bedroom, but she couldn't think about that now. That involved her ex, Frankie, and his twisted nurse fantasy. Somehow it didn't seem fair to Tim that her mind wandered to X-rated thoughts of another man.

"Good. I have a hat in the car. God knows my hair'll stand out like a tomato in a patch of snow."

His sometimes red, sometimes strawberry-blond hair made blending an issue. Plus, he was a big, handsome guy with that commanding presence some women, including Lucie, found sexy.

Tim tapped the map sitting on the table. "The money drop is at 11:00. Everyone be in place no later than 10:30. Dress warm, but conservatively. Yes, Ro, that means you."

"Oh, haha."

"I'm serious. Don't wear anything that makes you stand out."

Lucie eyed her. "Leave the leopard print coat here."

"Definitely," Tim said. "The goal is getting lost in the crowd. And I'm not sure how much of a crowd we'll have in a park in January. The fact that our perp actually picked this location leads me to think it's amateur hour."

"Good for us," Joey said.

"It is." Tim glanced up. "Is everyone set on their assignments?"

"Yep," Ro said. "*Blending*."

Jimmy offered a sarcastic salute. Dad cracked him on the back of the head, the two of them letting out a laugh.

What a crew.

"All right. Now the fun part. I'll show you all how to use the radios. Then we'll see you at the park. And whatever you do, don't call attention to yourselves."

LUCIE ENTERED CLIFFSIDE PARK AT 10:35. FIVE MINUTES behind schedule. Damned street parking.

Between the brisk walk and the sun's rays knocking the chill from the air, a few beads of sweat dripped from her neck. She tugged on the knot in her scarf, opening it enough for fresh air to hit her skin.

"You here?" Tim said in her ear via the handy-dandy radio.

She lifted her hand to check the wire at her ear. The one nicely hidden by her wig. All secure. Agent Lucie, ready for action. "I am. Sorry I'm late. Parking issues."

"You're fine. I'm on the bench three down from the one next to the tree."

Lucie followed the winding path that led to the target tree. She walked about 200 yards and spotted Tim in his baseball cap and sunglasses. He leaned forward, his big shoulders hunching as he propped his elbows on his knees and fiddled with his phone. With his hair covered and his body tucked under that puffy jacket, she almost didn't recognize him.

She glanced around, taking in the trees and dormant grass as she power-walked her way down the path. To anyone watching, she was simply a woman getting her daily 10,000 steps in. "Is everyone in place?"

"Yes," Tim said. "All good."

"Alpha Squad on alert."

Lucie rolled her eyes at Ro playing commando. In stilettos.

"Good lord," Lucie muttered, half laughing to herself.

"Roger," Mom said, "Dad and I are here with the girls."

Lucie glanced across the giant fountain where her parents strolled. Given Dad's weird celebrity status in Chicago, Lucie insisted he go incognito. They'd covered his trademark hair in a homburg-style hat and finished the look with dark sunglasses. Really, he looked like some sort of mobbed-up spy. But whatever. It got the job done.

"Jimmy?" she asked.

"I'm on the path. Trees are hiding me."

The gang's all here.

With everyone in place, Lucie continued down the path. She'd dressed accordingly for her power-walker role in yoga pants, sneakers, a winter athletic jacket, and, of course, her scarf and blond wig. Her mother barely recognized her, Antoine never would.

She hoofed by Tim, still on his bench, still messing with his phone. As she passed, he let out a wolf whistle.

Men. Such horndogs.

"Couldn't help it," he said via the radio.

"Well, try." She reminded herself to focus on the current predicament. "I'll do a spin around the fountain. Any sign of Antoine?"

"Not me," Jimmy said.

"No sightings by Alpha Squad."

"Wait," Mom said. "Who are we looking for?"

This is what happened when working with amateurs. "There will be a man by the bench two down from where Tim is. When we get closer to 11:00, Tim will walk off so Antoine doesn't recognize him."

"Got it," Mom said.

A couple of fellow power-walking women cruised along with slick looking jogging strollers. Lucie nodded, then checked over her shoulder making sure they were out of earshot before continuing. "Once Tim leaves, stay alert, but don't be obvious. Antoine will leave the money in that hollowed-out tree. He might still hang around though to watch for the blackmailer."

"I would," Dad said. "I'd take care of it right here."

"Kick their ass," Jimmy said.

"Everyone pipe down."

Thank you, Tim.

Three loud barks ensued. Sonny. Off to the right. Lucie swiveled her head around, found Jimmy and Sonny on the opposite side of the fountain. Sonny offered up a play bow to a Black Lab. How cute was he?

Jimmy, clearly staying on point, nudged him along. Also across the fountain, Joey and Ro entered the area with Otis lumbering along, head dipped low, clearly not amused by the new locale.

"Is Otis all right?"

"Yeah," Joey said. "He's tired. Mrs. L had company last night. He stayed up too late."

Damned parties. Poor Otis. "Maybe stand off to the side or something. Let him rest."

"He'll be fine."

"Alpha Squad out."

Someone snorted. Had to be Tim.

Lucie took the curve around the fountain, coming face-to-face with Mom, Dad, and the Ninja Bitches. The girls' heads snapped up. Despite the blond wig, they'd recognized her. So much for her disguise. Probably caught her scent. *Dang it.* As she drew closer, the girls leaped and tugged at their leashes, straining for some Lucie time.

Not now. So not Lucie time. When she ignored them, they barked. And barked. And barked.

"Luce," Tim said, "what the hell?"

"I know! I'm sorry. They must smell me."

"Well, go pet them or something. Shut them up."

Lucie hustled over, squatting to Ninja Bitch level and giving them both a good rub. "Girls," she said, sotto voce, "I love the greeting, but this is serious business here." Lucie smiled up at her parents, supposedly two people she didn't know. "What lovely dogs you have. And so friendly."

"They're too small for *me*," Dad said.

Blah, blah, whatever. Fannie leaped up, slathering Lucie with licks aplenty and knocking her off balance. If she didn't get up, she'd wind up ass over elbow. Talk about a spectacle.

Lucie stood, giving the girls one last pat. "It was nice meeting you, dogs, but I have to go."

Lucie continued on, picking up her pace and really getting into character by pumping her arms.

The far side of the fountain provided a straight-on view of the bench near the hollowed-out tree. She scanned the area, her gaze landing on Tim, who gave up on his phone and stood. He tucked his phone into his jacket pocket and moved away from his bench.

Showtime already? Lucie paused, pretending to read something on her phone while she checked the time. 10:55.

Any minute now Antoine would be entering the area.

"Stay alert, people," she said.

"Roger that."

"Got it."

"These Ninja Bitches are a handful."

"God help me," Tim muttered.

Why did Lucie have an overwhelming urge to apologize?

"Hang on," he said. "I think I see Antoine. At my 2:00. I gotta veer off or he'll see me. Luce, do you see him?"

She glanced up from her phone and found Chef Antoine entering the fountain area, casually strolling with his hands tucked into the straps of an oversized red backpack. "Yes. I see him."

"Good. I'll follow the path back around the fountain. Don't lose him."

A loud woof sounded—Otis. Lucie swung to Joey and Ro on the north side of the fountain, just yards from the drop point. Too close.

Joey stared down at Otis who had decided to siesta right on the path.

"Guys," Lucie said, "you have to move. Way too close. Antoine met Ro the other night. Even with her hat and scarf, he might recognize her."

Ro angled away from Antoine, giving her his back as he strode toward the bench. A young guy jogged toward them, then slowed to a walk as he checked his watch.

"Who's this now?" Lucie muttered.

"Don't know," Ro said, her voice hushed. "I'll get rid of him."

"No," Tim said. "He's a runner. He'll clear out after he checks his stats."

But Ro was already on the move, striding in the opposite direction toward the jogger.

Joey finally got Otis to his feet, but that stubborn animal wouldn't move. Just stood there like a tired old man. Dogs. So unpredictable.

"Luce," Tim said, "are you watching?"

She snapped back to Antoine, now sliding his backpack off and setting it on the bench. "Yes. Antoine's at the bench. Ro, *where* are you going?"

"Watch and learn, sister."

"Crap," Tim said.

"Language," Mom said.

Just as Ro neared the jogger, the extremely male and buff jogger, she drew up short, grabbing her calf. "Ooh, ow."

Lord, please no.

The jogger looked up at the hot brunette, apparently injured, and rushed over.

Men. Horndogs.

"Are you okay?" he said.

A chorus of voices erupted over the radio.

"What's wrong?"

"Who's hurt?"

"What the hell is going on?"

"I'm on my way."

Still with her eyes on Antoine, Lucie whipped her head sideways and spotted Jimmy rushing in from the cover of the trees.

"Jimmy, no. Stay back."

"Hey," Joey's voice.

Oh, no.

Lucie paused and did a half-turn, sliding her eyes to Ro and her fake injury then back to Antoine, who pushed off the bench. He grabbed his backpack and wandered to the tree, leaning on it.

"What hurts?"

That had to be the jogger. Lucie glanced over to where he squatted, his hands wrapped around Ro's calf.

Then Joey came into view and her head began to pound.

"Luce, focus!"

"I am. It's just—"

"Dude," Joey jerked his thumb, "hands off my girl."

And, yep, here we go.

"Huh?" the guy said, his hands still firmly planted on Ro's leg. "She's hurt, I'm trying to help."

"Yeah, well, you can do that without pawing at her. Hands. *Off*."

"Joey," Ro said. "Stop it. Why do you do this? All. The. Time. Always with the fighting. I swear you're a ten-year-old."

"Jeez, man. Don't be such an asshole."

"Crap," Tim said.

"I'm sorry," Lucie said.

Because really, she should have known better than to let Ro and Joey do an op together. They were too volatile.

"Excuse me," Mom said. "Did that man just call my son an asshole?"

Mom. Swearing. A panicked, choking laugh caught in Lucie's throat.

"Hold on." Dad's voice. "I'm coming over."

Sure. Why not throw a match on spilled gas? Lucie breathed in, fought through the banging in her skull. "No. Dad, please. Stay in position."

Antoine. She swung a look back where he slid the backpack from his shoulder and used his elbow to tuck it into the tree.

"Who're you calling an asshole? All I did was ask you to get your hands off her."

"Oh no. Tim, please, get over there before Joey pummels that guy."

"*Damn it.*"

Loud barking sounded. The Ninja Bitches doing their war cry as Mom and Dad descended on the soon-to-be bedlam involving their only son. The girls' growls came through the radio and Lucie's panic kicked up a notch.

"Mom, keep those dogs out of the fray. I'll kill someone if they get hurt."

Mom grabbed hold of the double leash, hanging back while Dad charged in and shoved the jogger.

"Oh for the love of God," Ro said. "You people!"

Look who was talking? The one who started the whole mess. Everything was fine and according to schedule until the drama queen showed up.

"Who're you pushing, old man?"

Uh-oh. "Tim?"

"I'm on it. Watch that tree."

And there he was, her hunky cop boyfriend darned near sprinting toward the group, ready to jump in and keep her father and brother from an assault charge.

Lucie swung back. No Antoine. *No, no, no.* She scanned the area, checking the five pathways leading to the fountain. Nothing.

Gone.

"Antoine's gone."

Giving up on Antoine, she turned back to the group. Tim inserted himself between Dad, Joey, and the jogger. "Whatever this is, everyone take a breath."

The jogger reached around Tim and shoved Joey. Not good. Even from across the fountain, the cold air became charged, the tension hanging like the blade of a guillotine about to drop. Her moose of a brother almost came out of his shoes lunging at the guy. With Tim in the middle.

He gripped Joey's jacket, threw all his weight into him, and shoved him back a step.

"Tim," Lucie said, "I'd get out of there."

"Damn it, Joey, calm down."

The tree.

The money.

Lucie looked back. No one.

Except...

A young guy wearing jeans, a black puffy jacket, and a beanie cap headed down the path toward the park exit. Where'd he come from?

A red backpack hung on his shoulder.

Behind her, Tim continued doing his magic, separating Joey and the jogger while keeping Jimmy and Dad from jumping in.

Backpack.

Before beanie boy got too far, Lucie started walking, her sneaker clad feet pounding the asphalt as she hustled to catch up.

"Someone just picked up the backpack. It's a guy wearing a black jacket and beanie cap. I'm following him."

"Luce, wait."

"I've got this. Just follow me. I'll distract him long enough for you to catch up and grab him."

"You," Tim said to the jogger, "beat it. Get out of here now before you get the crap kicked out of you by Joe Rizzo's son."

Who knew Tim was such a namedropper? A pause ensued. She stole a quick glance at her family.

The jogger put his hands up. "J-Joe *Rizzo*?"

"The one and only," Tim said.

"Shit. O-okkay. Sorry. Sorry. Didn't mean any disrespect. Lady, I hope your leg is okay."

"Beat it," Tim hollered, his voice tight enough to strangle an elephant.

Her man was about to lose his hot Irish temper.

Backpack.

Lucie picked up her pace, following the path into the trees, out of sight of her family.

"Luce? Where are you?"

"I'm on the path heading to the exit. This guy is moving quick, so hurry. "

Beanie Boy reached the park exit and Lucie broke into a dead run, chasing him down, keeping him in sight as he raised his arm. She drew closer, maybe twelve feet away. A black sedan eased to the curb. Beanie Boy stepped back, waiting for the car to stop.

No.

If he got into that car, the money would be gone. He opened the door and Lucie's panic hit hyper-drive. Still running, a fierce blood rush blurred her vision. She blinked a couple of times, set her mind on the task of focusing.

Do something.

She ran harder, her feet slamming against the pavement, sending shocks of pain up her legs. But Beanie Boy was right there. Just feet in front of her. *Stop him.* Her breaths came in short, angry bursts. She leaped, her arms outstretched as she flew. *Boom!* She slammed into the guy.

"What the...hey, watch it lady!"

Lucie careened off him, plowing into the doorframe, the impact nearly tearing her torso apart. Her head snapped sideways. The force knocked her wig askew and her earpiece loose. She landed half on the back seat, her lower body hanging off. Quickly, she pressed her finger to her ear, securing the earpiece.

"Get her out," the driver yelled.

No, sir. *Uh-huh.* They weren't leaving with that money. Lucie poked a finger. "I want that backpack."

"Luce!"

Tim's voice. Not in her ear. Coming from the park. Beanie Boy spun around. Lucie followed his gaze to where Tim sprinted toward them.

Something clamped on to the back of Lucie's coat. The driver. Hauling her into the car. She reared back, smacked at the arm of a big, beefy guy.

"Get in and you won't get hurt."

Lucie grabbed on to the doorframe, pulling against it for resistance. "Ha! Are you kidding me? The victim should never allow herself to be taken to a second location. Tim!"

The young guy with the backpack grabbed her feet. She kicked out, got him in the shoulder.

"Ow," he said. "Stop it. Just get in."

He locked one arm around her legs, lassoing them. He shoved and her grip loosened on the doorframe. Another bout of panic exploded. If they got her into that car, it was over.

Beanie Boy shoved again and the driver came half over the seat, grabbing her with both hands. *Ohmigod. Too much.* The force was too much. Her fingers slid and Beanie Boy pushed and...no.

She lost her grip.

Momentum rolled her backward, flopping her onto the floorboard. Seconds. That's all it took to get her into that car. The self-defense gurus would be mortified.

She smacked her hand against the back of the front seat. "Let me out!"

Beanie Boy hopped in and slammed the door. "Go."

Lucie kicked out again, landed a blow to his shoulder this time. "Ow. Quit it. I won't hurt you."

"Let me out of this car."

She kicked him again. Couldn't hurt.

He shifted sideways, his back against the door, and held his hands up. "Can't. You shouldn't have come after me. What the hell are you doing anyway?"

These idiots had no idea how bad they'd just screwed

up. "Morons," she screamed. "Antoine thinks I'm the black-mailer. If I let that money disappear, I'll never clear myself."

"This was supposed to be an easy job," the driver said, his voice flat and totally unaffected.

"Kidnapping," Lucie cried. "You're kidnapping me. Federal offense!"

"Technically," the driver said, "it's abduction."

Verbal swordplay? Now?

"Whatever. You're doing it, and guess what? That big guy screaming my name? He's my boyfriend. And he's a Chicago cop. A *detective*. You guys are toast."

"Luce," Tim said in her ear, "I'm right behind you. In a cab. Don't let them see the radio."

Whew. She fought the urge to look out the rear window, to see him and know that he was with her. That he'd take care of her.

I can do this.

Still on the floor, she wiggled to a sitting position and smoothed a hand over her wig, giving it a surreptitious straightening while making sure it covered her ear and the radio hooked around it.

Beanie Boy pushed his hands into his forehead. "I need to think."

"You'd better think about letting me go before this gets worse."

Lucie scooted back, closer to the rear driver's side door. Maybe, when they stopped for a light, she could roll out. Make a run for Tim just behind them.

The clunk of door locks sounded. "Nice try," the driver said. "Child safety locks are now on. You're not going anywhere."

13

"Baby girl?" Dad's voice streamed through the earpiece. "Are you okay?"

Um, no. Not okay. She'd just been kidnapped. Of course she wasn't okay.

"She can't answer," Tim said. "They'll know she has a radio."

Thank you, O'Hottie.

Tiny prickles traveled along the bottoms of her feet. Being crunched on the floorboard inhibited her circulation. She looked up at her abductor. "Can I move to the seat?"

"Yeah. Sure."

"Tim," Joey said, "we just got to the car." His voice held a breathy edge as if he'd sprinted a mile. "Where are you?"

"About to jump on Lake Shore. She's in a black Lincoln Continental. I'm calling it in."

"No!" The word flew from her mouth—*dang it*—and Beanie Boy narrowed his eyes. *Uh-oh. Think fast.* She kicked him in the thigh. "No! You can't take me."

In the world of fast thinking, it wasn't great, but Beanie Boy simply rubbed his thigh.

"Hey, take it easy."

"I'm sorry, Luce," Tim said. "We're beyond a blackmail scheme. Way beyond. If I hadn't run after you, we wouldn't even know where you are right now."

"Call it in," Dad said. "I want these guys fried."

The driver cruised down Lake Shore, obviously sticking close to the speed limit.

Lucie sat forward. "Listen, driver, you can still pull over. Just let me out and I'll forget this whole thing. Take the money, I don't care."

"Oh," the driver said, "we're taking the money. As soon as I dump you two off, I'm taking my cut and I'm gone."

Greedy little bugger. But, hey, she'd learned a few things growing up in Villa Rizzo. She waved her hand, got his attention via the rearview. "What are they paying you? I'll double it if you let me go."

"Fifty grand."

Fifty! *Wow*. She was in the wrong line of work. "Fine. $100,000 if you let me out."

Not that she had that kind of money to spare, but he didn't know that. Plus, Dad probably had bricks of cash stashed in the attic.

"Shut up," Beanie Boy said.

"Baby girl, do these dumbasses know who they're messing with?"

"Good point."

She winced. Dad had to stop talking to her before he got her killed. Or worse. She faced Beanie Boy. "Hey, genius. Do you even know who I am?"

He rolled his eyes. "The mayor's kid?"

"Ha. Very funny. You should be so lucky. Try Joe Rizzo's kid."

"Joe Rizzo?"

Lord, leave it to her to find the only kidnapper in Chicago who didn't know who Joe Rizzo was.

"What?" The driver screamed.

Blood surged and for the first time, Lucie experienced the full weight of throwing her father's name around. Not that it was anything to be proud of, but if it got her out of this car, she'd leverage it as far as she could.

"Yep. Joe Rizzo. *That* Joe Rizzo. He was in the park, you know. Probably saw this whole thing. And, just so you know, he's *extremely* protective. Emphasis on extremely."

A loud, deep *woof* sounded in her ear.

Dear God, they had Otis with them. Where were the girls?

Beanie Boy whipped out his phone.

"Who're you calling?" Lucie asked.

"None of your business. And stop talking. You're the prisoner, you don't get to talk."

Oh, she'd talk. If only to rattle these two.

"Keep talking, Luce," Tim said.

"It's me," Beanie Boy said into his phone.

Lucie leaned toward him, hoping to horn in on his conversation with whoever sat at the other end of the line.

The guy shoved her back. "Go away." He went back to his call. "She just said she's Joe Rizzo's daughter."

"*The* Joe Rizzo," Lucie announced.

"Whoever the hell he is."

"Seriously?" Tim said.

Female yelling streamed from the other end of Beanie Boy's phone.

"Quit screaming. What was I supposed to do? She ran after me at the park and your goon friend pulled her into the car. Now she won't shut up."

Beanie Boy pressed his free hand into his forehead

again. "What should I do?...Okay...You're sure?...Okay." He disconnected and looked at the driver. "We're going to the office."

In the rearview, Lucie caught the driver's eyebrows shoot up. "The *office*?"

"That's what she said. She knows what she's doing."

Lucie met Beanie Boy's eye. "What office?"

"You'll find out soon enough. Now be quiet."

"It's okay, Luce." Tim said. "I'm with you."

"We're all with you," Joey said. "I've got Mom and Dad in the car. The dogs, too."

This might take some explaining to Mrs. L and the Bernards. *Gee, sorry your sweet babies rode shotgun on an abduction rescue.*

Lucie sat back and let out a long breath. If nothing else, wherever they were going, she'd soon know who the blackmailer was.

TIM RODE IN THE BACK OF THE CAB, HIS HEAD SWIVELING TO check the alleys and side streets in search of the Lincoln they'd just lost at a stop light. Lucie, for the first time in her life, had gone silent.

"Luce? Where are you?"

The line stayed quiet, but she let out a heavy sigh, letting him know she'd heard him.

Good. Still there.

Can't talk.

"When it's safe, let me know where you are."

She coughed. "Oh, look," she said. "One of the Cubs is doing a book signing at Gillespie's. I'm a huge Cubs fan."

Gillespie's. The big independent bookstore. Back when

he was a rookie, he'd cruised that neighborhood thousands of times. "Make a left," he directed the cab driver.

"Sure. Who we chasing?"

In the tradition of psycho Chicago cab drivers, the guy hit his brakes way too late and swung the turn, nearly fishtailing the car.

"Thanks," Tim said, ignoring the driver's question. "Just stay straight. I'll tell you when to turn again."

Seconds ticked to minutes and his pulse hammered, the *bhum-bhum-bhum* reminding him Lucie had been taken hostage.

An agonizing five minutes passed as visions of his sweet, funny Lucie strapped to a chair filled his mind.

"Luce? Breathe or cough or something. Please, let me know you're there."

"Huh," she said. "Molly's office? Why are we at *Molly's*?"

That set Tim back some. Jacardi's office. Huh, was right.

The cab driver jerked to a halt at a stop sign then swung back to look at Tim. "Where to now?"

If Tim survived this cab ride without winding up in traction, it'd be a miracle. And he was a cop used to defensive driving.

He pointed. "Make a left. Then stop at the next corner. I'm hopping out."

"Really?"

Tim dug into his wallet, praying he had enough cash to cover the ride. Otherwise, he'd be handing over his credit card and running. "Yeah. How much?"

The driver, an older man with shaggy gray hair and glasses, rolled his bottom lip out. Seriously? The guy was pouting.

"I can keep driving," he said. "No charge."

"That's okay. Thanks though. Appreciate it." Tim

checked the meter. Twenty-eight bucks. He could do that. He tossed a couple twenties over the seat and reached for the door handle.

Molly's office was three blocks west, but they were city blocks and he'd get there faster on foot. He picked up his pace while calling in Lucie's abduction. Later, he'd have a boatload of explaining to do, but currently he needed to manage this situation.

Cars lined the street in both directions, so he jaywalked, jockeying between the lanes.

A cabbie rolled down his window and shouted something in Spanish. Tim held up a meaculpa wave. "Joey? Did you get that? Molly Jacardi's office. Where are you?"

"I'm on it. We'll be there in two minutes."

"Okay. Don't go in. Do *not*."

"Why?"

He'd need a week to explain all the ways it could go wrong. Possible weapons, all of them taken hostage, perp panicking and shooting up the place.

Or killing himself by blowing his head clear off in front of Lucie.

The thought twisted Tim's gut. Having seen suicide victims and the ensuing result, he knew she'd never recover from that. He sure as hell hadn't.

"Get out," a male voice came through the radio.

Kidnapper.

"Are we going inside?" Lucie asked.

"Yeah. Now shut up and move."

Good girl. She'd kept her head about her and fed him information without tipping them off that she had a radio clipped to the inside of her sleeve.

He turned right on Molly's block. A horn honked and he peered left, but kept running as Joey's Jeep slowed to a crawl in the middle of the street. Lucie's father sat in the passenger seat. Ro and Mrs. Rizzo in the back. The dogs had to be in the cargo area.

"We're goin' in," Lucie's father said.

Tim anticipated that. Joe Rizzo wasn't about to let his daughter be taken hostage. Tim kept running. If he stopped, he'd lose time. With Lucie in trouble, he couldn't have that. Not today. He drew a long breath of cold, winter air. Let the chill settle in his lungs for a few seconds before he exhaled. *Patience.* Dealing with this crew took every ounce.

He met Joe Sr.'s direct and challenging glare. "You're going in? Great. Then you'll all be taken hostage. Trust me on this. Stay outside. I've already called it in. SWAT is on the way. They'll take care of it and nobody gets hurt."

"If anyone gets hurt," Joe Sr. said, it won't be us.

Finally, Tim stopped running and Joey hit the brakes. Tim walked to the car and held a finger up. "You have no idea what you're walking into. All we have is ears. We can't see if there's a gun or the office is wired with explosives. We know none of that. All due respect, but you're not going in. I don't care if I have to handcuff you to a light pole. I'll go in alone."

Joe's cheeks hardened and a red flush drenched his face. "She's my daughter. I'm not leaving her in there."

"Of course not. But you going in won't help her. Please, trust me on this. I love her. If I thought you busting in would fix it, we'd all go in. I was just there yesterday. They know I'm a cop. I'll act like I'm doing another check and walk right in."

AFTER SENDING THE DRIVER ON HIS WAY, BEANIE BOY SHOVED

Lucie through the door. She stumbled inside, momentum carrying her to the empty receptionist's desk. She locked onto to the edge and righted herself. The top of the desk was clear of any folders or papers. If someone was working there today, they sure were neat about it.

Lucie stood tall, pushed her shoulders back. In times like this, Rizzos didn't show fear. Or weakness. Predators pounced on weakness. "Where's the receptionist?"

"Day off, I guess." He grabbed Lucie by the elbow and held her in place while he peered down the hallway. "We're here!"

A second later, the clunk of a door handle disengaging sounded and Molly stepped out of her office. She wore her typical high-end suit and her honey-blond hair had been pulled back into a French twist. Formidable. That's how she looked.

Well, she wasn't the only one.

Molly stared at Lucie in the stupid blond wig. "Lucie? Is that you?" She glanced at Beanie Boy, her eyes a little wary. "Who're you? What's going on?"

Lucie gawked. Seriously? She dragged her back here, pretending to have no idea it was happening? After they found that recipe in her office?

Puh-lease.

"What's going on," Lucie said, "is your henchman took me hostage. That's criminal! God, I knew it was you. You should be ashamed of yourself. Trying to blame me for this."

Molly's head snapped back. "What *are* you talking about?"

Now she wanted to play dumb?

"Nice try, Molly. I was at the park. Watching the drop. You didn't think I was going to just sit back and let this

ADRIENNE GIORDANO

happen, did you? I'm not taking the blame while you walk off with Antoine's money. No way."

She took a step, but Beanie Boy gripped her elbow, holding her.

"Annalise!" Molly said. "Call the police. Lucie Rizzo is here making ridiculous accusations."

Annalise rushed into the hallway, her long hair flying. She spotted Beanie Boy holding onto Lucie and stopped short. "Lucie? What are you doing?"

Another one. Terrific. "Ha! It's not about me. *Molly* is the one. She has Antoine's recipe behind her bookcase."

Molly did that head-snapping thing again. What an actress. "What recipe?"

Lucie ignored her and focused on Annalise. Naturally, the assistant's loyalties would be to her boss, but Lucie and Annalise had a lot in common. In an odd way, they'd bonded over their brief meeting the other day. They understood each other.

"Annalise, she's setting me up. Look behind the bookcase. The recipe is taped there. And this guy," Lucie jerked her thumb at Beanie Boy, "just picked up the money at the ransom drop. At first, I thought Reuben was the blackmailer."

Molly's mouth dropped open. "This is so bizarre. *Reuben?* Why would you think that? He's the most decent person I know."

"Well, because he's mad at Antoine."

"How do you know that?"

Whoopsie. Perhaps Lucie should learn to control her mouth or she'd wind up copping to hacking into Antoine's email.

"There is no recipe behind my bookcase," Molly continued. "I'm the one concerned about hard copies in Antoine's safe. I certainly wouldn't keep one behind my office furniture."

Annalise perked up. "I'm not sure what Lucie is talking about, but it seems to me there's one way to figure it out." She spun on her low heels and strode to Molly's office. "Let's look behind the bookcase. When there's nothing there, we'll know Lucie is lying."

Oh, these women. Lucie curled her fingers into tight fists, ready to pummel something. Calm. She needed to remain calm. Tim would be here any second.

She'd be fine.

Just fine.

She opened her hands, stretched her fingers, then pointed. "Unless Molly moved it, it's back there."

"And you know this how?"

Oh, boy. "I'm not at liberty to say. But it's there. Trust me."

Trust me? That was a dumb thing to say. Clearly, they didn't trust her if they thought she blackmailed their client. Whatever. After this episode, she might need psychotherapy. At the very least, anger management after she went crazy on these people for accusing her of being a thief.

Annalise marched into the office followed by Molly. Lucie started walking. Beanie Boy gripped her elbow tighter and she tugged away. "Get off me. I'm going to watch Annalise pull that recipe from behind Molly's bookcase. After what this woman has put me through, I'm not risking her hiding anything."

Molly handed Annalise a flashlight so she could see behind the giant bookcase.

Lucie pointed. "It's closer to the window."

Molly shook her head. "Believe me. There's nothing back there."

"Um, Molly," Annalise said. "There's something back there."

TIM STOOD AT THE SIDE OF MOLLY JACARDI'S BUILDING huddled with Team Rizzo. Team Rizzo and the dogs. One of the Ninja Bitches squatted and took a dump that no dog that small should be able to accomplish.

Lucie's mom stared down at the pile, frowning. "I might as well clean this up. It'll give me *something* to do." She slid a poop bag from the holder on the leash. "Good girl, Josie. Lucie would be proud."

What a cluster.

The first cruiser pulled to the curb and, hearing the tick of the engine, Tim turned.

"Great," Joe Sr. said. "Cops."

Mrs. Rizzo finished with the poop, tied a knot at the end of the bag, and swung it at her husband. "You shush! Our girl is in there. I don't care who gets her out as long as she gets out."

Before the shit went flying—literally—Tim held up his hands. "Please. Stay calm. I'm gonna talk to these guys. All of you stay here." He met the eye of each of them, then focused on Joey. Out of this bunch, the only one Tim thought had a remote shot at staying calm was Joey. Go figure. Biggest hothead around, but he had a strategic mind.

"I'm on it," Joey said. "Go."

"Thank you." Tim held out his hands. "I need the radios. All of them."

Mrs. R's eyes went wide. "Absolutely not. I need to know what's going on in there."

Precisely why he wanted the radios back. He'd seen

enough of these situations to know they could go bad fast. And he'd didn't want Lucie's family, her very high-strung and reactive family, listening if—or when—it did.

Bad enough he had to listen to the woman he loved being held hostage. Her parents? Not a chance.

He met Joey's eye again. *Come on, Joey. Think.*

Joey reached up, unhooked his earpiece, then held out his hands. "Everyone, fork 'em over. Tim's right."

A trio of voices merged, all of them offering up reasons why they should be allowed to keep the radios. Finally, Joey whistled, the sound ear-splitting enough to send the dogs into a barking frenzy.

Tim didn't know what it was with the Rizzos, but they created chaos. Always.

"Gang," Tim said, "we're wasting time here. SWAT is on the way. Right now, these radios are our only communication with her. SWAT should have them. For Lucie's safety."

Joey, still holding his hands out, jerked his chin at Ro and his parents. "Hand 'em over. Right now."

Each of them tugged their earpieces free, grumbling over the injustice. In seconds, Tim had confiscated all the devices and shoved them in his jacket pockets.

"Telling you right now," Joe Sr. said, "If I don't like the way this looks, I'm goin' in there. These cops can shoot me if they want. I don't care."

"Understood."

Tim jogged over to the police cruiser and flashed his badge. Two cops hopped out just as the second cruiser swung around the corner, parking in the fire zone Ro had utilized the other day.

"I called it in," Tim said. "My girlfriend, Lucie Rizzo, is being held inside. So far, it's been non-violent."

The cop used his hand to block the sun as he studied the building. "Give me the particulars."

Did this guy have ten years?

Before Tim could launch into an explanation, another unmarked and thoroughly beat up Chevy pulled up, squeezing into the fire zone behind the cruiser. A stocky guy with short, graying hair slid out. He wore gray dress slacks that bagged at the ankles and a faded oxford shirt under a long wool coat. He approached Tim and the uniformed cop.

Not wanting to waste time, Tim held up his badge. "Tim O'Brien."

The guy studied his creds then held up his own badge. "Curt King. I'm the negotiator."

"You got here fast."

"Yeah. I was only a couple of blocks away." He faced the uniformed officers. "Set up a perimeter while we're waiting on SWAT. Someone take the back of the building. Make sure no one flees."

Orders delivered, the uniformed cops marched off. Curt studied the office building, doing a visual sweep of the front. "What have we got here?"

Tim spent a few minutes bringing the negotiator up to speed, stopping to answer questions when needed and providing the need-to-know facts. Some of the ancillary facts—like Joey impersonating a cable guy—Curt didn't need.

When Tim was through, Curt let out a long breath. "Does your lieutenant know you're involved in this?"

Tim shook his head. "No. I took a personal day. Was hoping to keep it quiet. In my own defense, I urged the chef to call the police. He didn't want law enforcement involved. The only reason I'm involved is Lucie."

"Love is a many splendored thing."

"Amen, brother."

"Awright." Curt gestured to the building with his pen. "They're all inside?"

"Yes."

Curt checked his notes. "And this is Molly Jacardi's office?"

"Yeah. Normally there's a receptionist at the desk. According to what we heard on the radio, she's not there. So far, we have Jacardi, her assistant, Annalise, and the guy that shoved Lucie into the car."

"Do we know who he is?"

"Not a clue. Not even a name."

"Okay. Lucie still has the radio?"

"Yeah." Tim reached into his pockets for the devices "Here. There's four of them. Earpieces and the mics."

Curt rolled his bottom lip. "Pretty slick."

"We went with the easily concealable ones. Buddy of mine had them."

"This is good." He shoved one of the earpieces into his ear and spoke into the mic. "Lucie? This is Lieutenant Curt King of the Chicago Police Department. Can you hear me? If so, clear your throat."

Lucie cleared her throat. "Good. We're going to get you out. Try and stay calm. Is everyone all right? If so, clear your throat."

Another throat clearing.

Hearing her signal, the churning in Tim's belly settled. He let out a long breath, realizing that yes, despite his normally stressful job, being personally involved took more energy to wrap his mind around. To control his emotions.

"Good." Curt said. "In a few minutes, I'm going to attempt to make contact and resolve this quickly. Stay calm. We're here for you."

Curt clicked off and headed back toward his car. "I'm gonna call the landline and see if they'll answer."

"Whoa!" One of the cops yelled from somewhere behind Tim. "You can't go in there!"

Tim whirled around and...shit. Team Rizzo was on the move. Lucie's father led the charge, followed by Joey—the one Tim counted on. Trailing behind were Ro and Mrs. Rizzo, both holding leashes. Every one of them—dogs included—hustling along the sidewalk.

Toward the office's main entrance.

Tim broke into a run, his feet pounding the pavement hard enough to send tiny shocks up his legs.

"Joe! Stop!"

Damn it. He wouldn't get there in time. They had too much of a jump on him. One of the cops made an attempt to intercede. Joey halted, sidestepped out of formation, making himself a human wall. *Boom!* The cop plowed into the mountain known as Joe Rizzo Jr., his arms cycling as he landed flat on his ass.

"Joey," Tim called, "stop them. Don't!" Joe Sr., reached the door, swung it open, and—*crap*—stepped through.

One by one, each of them hustled through the door while Tim stood there helplessly.

Go in.

No. Stupid idea. As much as he'd love to bust in and settle this whole thing, going in meant giving Molly Jacardi more leverage.

Thirty seconds ago she had one hostage.

Now she had five.

And three dogs.

14

"OF COURSE THERE'S SOMETHING BACK THERE," LUCIE SAID AS Anna worked her rail thin arm behind the bookcase.

Unfortunately, Lucie couldn't elaborate on why she was so positive. But she'd seen it herself via Joey's spy glasses.

Anna squished the side of her face against the bookcase. "I've...almost...got...it."

The idiot who'd abducted Lucie stood by while Annalise struggled. Lucie turned and swatted his arm. "Hey, how about helping her? Move the bookcase."

"I don't understand what's going on here," Molly said.

Right. That's what they all said. Lucie had heard it a million times. Sometimes from her own family.

"Baby girl!"

Dad? What the...

Lucie angled to the door, staring at the empty space, dumbfounded. Lucie's crack kidnappers hadn't locked the front door.

"Dad?"

Before Lucie could move, her family piled into the office,

each falling in behind, one right after the other. Dad, Joey, Ro, and Mom.

Otis and the Ninja Bitches.

Lucie gasped. How would she explain this one to Mrs. L and the Bernards? She flapped her arms. "Are you crazy bringing those dogs in here? This is a hostage situation."

"Got it," Annalise said.

She eased her arm from behind the bookcase and held up the envelope Joey had found.

All eyes went to Molly. She stood stock still, her gaze glued to that envelope. A few seconds in, as if the situation had finally broken through, her mouth slid open. "That is *not* mine. I have no idea what it is."

"That's easy," Joey said. "It's the recipe you tried to frame my sister with."

"Nobody move."

Tim's voice. Now *he* was in here? Once again, Lucie angled back. Her man stood in the doorway, his gun drawn.

"Whoa," Beanie Boy said. "I didn't sign up for guns."

Lucie waved at the envelope in Annalise's hand. "That's the recipe. Annalise just dug it out."

"I didn't put that there," Molly cried. "Why would I do that? Antoine's my client. I made ten million last year on that recipe. It's worth more as a secret. Why would I risk that for a measly, one-time two million dollars?"

A measly two million? Rich people. Unbelievable.

But...huh. She had a point. Anyone with half a brain could see that.

"Chicago PD! We're coming in."

Tim poked his head out the door. "We're in here, Curt."

Ah, the hostage negotiator who'd introduced himself to Lucie a few minutes ago. Good. Maybe he could get to the bottom of this.

"We should call Antoine," Anna said. "He needs to know about this. About Molly blackmailing him."

"I didn't!"

At Molly's tone, the Ninja Bitches stood. Both their tails were up. Hyper-alert. Lucie had seen this before when one of them felt threatened.

Fannie let out a low growl.

Lucie shifted closer to Mom, casually taking the leash before the girls went crazy on Molly and took off a leg.

"It's all right, girls. She's not yelling at you. Don't get crazy."

"This is ridiculous." Molly walked to the phone. "I'll call Antoine myself."

"Put the phone down," the lieutenant said.

A heated stare down ensued. At least until the lieutenant pulled out a set of handcuffs.

Molly slammed the phone down, the *thwack* splitting the tension like a log. The girls lunged and let out three rapid-fire barks. Otis, taking his cue, hopped to his feet, bumping Ro with all of his eighty-five pounds. He knocked her sideways and she wobbled on her stilettos. Her *walking* shoes.

On her way to the floor, Ro bumped Mom, whose motherly instinct flared. She reached for Ro, but Ro, with too much momentum dragged them both down. Lucie dropped the leash and lunged for her mother.

Which only intensified the girls' reaction. They took off, straight to Molly, with Otis joining the effort. All three of them charged as Ro hit the ground.

"Otis, girls, no!"

Molly put her arms up and the girls skidded to a stop, but...uh-oh. *Too late.*

Boom. Otis leaped and barreled into her. She tipped

backward, slamming into the side of her desk before toppling over and landing on her stomach. Otis jumped on her back and Molly let out a grunt.

The big boy stood, head up, pinning Molly to the ground. He stared at Lucie with *look-what-I-did* pride on full display.

Ro slammed her hand on the floor. "These damned dogs. I'm definitely going to have a bruise." Joey helped her to her feet.

Curt shot Tim a look. "Is this normal?"

Ha. The good lieutenant had no idea.

"This?" Tim said casually. "This is a cakewalk."

Wait. Lucie spun around, scanned everyone still in the office. "Where's Beanie Boy?"

Tim was already in motion when Annalise's shoulders flew back. Her gaze shot to the door. "He still has the money. Get him!"

"I've got the front," Tim said. "Take the back."

Curt went right toward the back door and everyone filed out, half the group chasing Tim and the other half Curt.

At the front door, Lucie stopped short.

The recipe. Annalise still had it and Lucie didn't want it disappearing. Not when she'd been suspected of stealing it.

She turned, spotted Molly, Joey and Ro going out the back door.

No Anna. And she hadn't been with the group following Tim.

Wait.

One.

Second.

Lucie tip-toed back to Molly's office. *No Anna.* A quiet charge lit the air, making Lucie's skin itch. She hovered close to the wall, moving to the next office. Annalise's. The door was open. Lucie halted just outside. Listening.

The sound of rustling paper drifted to the hallway. Why was Anna standing around when everyone else went after the money? What would be so important that she'd let a man run off with her client's two million dollars?

Unless...

Did Anna already know what the outcome would be?

A weird sickness filled Lucie. All this time, they'd been focusing on Molly when Annalise had also been at Antoine's that day.

Oh, no.

Wait, wait, wait.

Lucie would not do this. All her life she'd been fighting assumptions about her character. One thing she would not do was judge Annalise. Not when she didn't have proof.

Get the proof.

She pushed off the wall with a quick half spin, planted her hands on the doorframe, and blocked the exit. Annalise stood at her desk, recipe card in hand, the envelope nowhere to be seen.

On the desk sat a briefcase with Anna's coat haphazardly thrown over it. Was she ready to leave? To take off? *Vamoose.*

Anna brought her gaze up. Their eyes locked. The only sound was the whir of the ceiling fan that stirred the thick air.

Finally, Anna nodded. "Lucie, hi. I thought you ran out with the others."

I bet you did.

"I started to. Then I realized I didn't see you. I wondered where you were."

Anna glanced at the recipe card still in her hand then held it up. "I was afraid something would happen to the recipe. I wanted to make sure it got back to Antoine."

Sure she did. *Damn it.* All this time, they'd suspected Molly when it could have been Anna.

Or both.

"Did you now?"

Anna cocked her head. "Of course. He's my client. I'd do anything for him."

"Because you're the responsible one, right?"

Now it all started to make sense. Lucie tightened her grip on the doorframe. Anna wasn't leaving until Lucie knew the truth.

Anna's brows drew together. "I'm sorry?"

"When I asked you for help with Molly, you told me you had always been the responsible one in your family. Taking care of your brother because your mother couldn't. How you were determined to make your own way. Just like me."

"Well, sure. What's your point?"

"The recipe."

"What about it?"

"How did you ever think you'd get away with stealing it?"

TIM HIT THE SIDEWALK IN A DEAD RUN, HIS GAZE PING-ponging as he searched the surrounding area for a kid with a backpack. Following him were Joey and Roseanne, but, in those stupid high heels, Ro fell behind. Just as well. Tim could only handle so much crazy.

There. To the right. One of the uniformed cops was in motion, running hard. Tim spotted a flash of red. Backpack.

He hauled ass, cutting diagonally across the street with Joey on his heels.

Tim pointed. "There. You see him?"

"Got it. I'll take the alley, see if we can cut him off on the next block."

"Go."

At the corner, Tim crossed again, running in the street alongside the row of parked cars to avoid pedestrians slowing him down. On the opposite side, the cop lost ground on their perp, so Tim stepped it up, his feet flying over pavement. Whichever way this guy turned, they had him. Joey from the left and Tim from the right.

If he went straight...

Deal with it then.

"Hold it," The cop yelled.

The kid glanced back. Big mistake. That look back just cost him precious seconds. Between the chase and flowing adrenaline, Tim's heart slammed. The sounds of traffic and car horns faded, and his sharp breaths echoed in his ears.

Slow the breathing down.

He inhaled through his nose and slowly let it out his mouth. Fifty yards ahead, the traffic light flipped to amber. Perfect. In a few seconds, the cross street would have the green and cars—if Tim knew Chicago traffic at all—would roar through that intersection taking out anything in their path.

His subject had limited choices. Run into traffic and get pancaked, or turn.

Twenty-five yards. *Come on, dude. Come my way.*

A passing driver honked and Tim nudged closer to the line of parked cars. Ten yards.

Come on. Come on.

Decision time.

Dude stopped. *Yes.* He jerked his head left, where Joey steamed straight toward him, and hooked a right, darting into the street.

That brief hesitation gave Tim an extra few seconds and he pumped his legs as the car that honked at him pulled alongside, aiming to make a right on red.

He smacked a hand against the window. "Wait!"

Damn it. The kid might just beat him to the corner. Unless...

Crap. This was gonna hurt. His football days roared back to him and he slid a gaze to the car, now at a full stop to his left. *Thank you.* He cleared the front of the car and braced himself.

One, two, three.

He left the ground, his body sailing. The kid whipped his head right and his face contorted, his lips peeling back as he prepared for the tackle.

Whack. Tim slammed into the smaller man, the two of them crashing to the blacktop. A car on the cross street swerved, the driver hitting the horn as Tim and the kid rolled into the middle of the intersection, both landing on their backs.

Of all the ways Tim imagined dying, this wasn't one of them.

All traffic stopped. A woman somewhere behind them let out a scream.

"Hold it," the cop yelled.

Apparently, the kid needed a hearing test because he hopped up, ready to run. Tim scrambled to his feet, grabbed the back of the kid's jacket.

"Don't be stupid," he said.

The kid swung an elbow and Tim ducked. So much for good advice. "Now you're pissing me off."

Outweighing the kid by at least thirty pounds, he gripped the jacket tighter, hooked the fingers of his free hand into one of the kid's belt loops, and shoved him to the ground.

"Stay there."

To ensure cooperation, Tim dropped one knee to the kid's back.

His breaths came hard and he forced himself to inhale slowly. In and out. In and out.

The cop came to a stop, his hands automatically going to his thighs as Joey joined the party.

"Cuff him," Tim said.

The cop unhooked his cuffs, and Tim gave the kid a light smack on the shoulder. "I'm gonna get up. Don't try anything stupid. There's three of us. All bigger than you."

The kid's head bobbed up and down. "I won't. This is all my sister's fault. All she said was to pick up the backpack. That's all."

"Who's your sister?"

"Anna."

"Annalise? Molly's assistant."

"Yeah. She said she had the whole thing worked out."

———

"*STEALING* IT," ANNA SAID, HER VOICE FILLED WITH ENOUGH indignation to start a small war. "Lucie, did you hit your head or something? I just told you I wanted to get it back to Antoine."

She scooped up her coat and slid it on before zipping the recipe card into the front pocket of her briefcase.

"Great," Lucie said. "I'll go with you. We can tell him all

about how *Molly,* his own girlfriend—and let's not forget, business manager—tried to blackmail him."

Anna hooked the briefcase over her shoulder and headed to the door. "You're not coming."

Still centered in the doorway, Lucie stared up at Anna, a good seven inches taller.

"Move," Anna said.

Lucie slid to the side, but if it took her jumping on Anna's back, she'd be tagging along. "Sure. We'll have to take your car. What with me being kidnapped from the park and all."

"I repeat, you're not coming. This is a private meeting between me and my client. You understand."

"Sister," Lucie said, "not in this lifetime will I ever understand. So, *we* will go see your client. Once he is confident I didn't take his recipe, you can have your private time."

Anna's nostrils flared wide. A low growl sounded in her throat.

If she thought this was frustrating, she had a lot to learn about life with Lucie Rizzo and company.

Lucie smiled. "Shall we go?"

Then she did it. Just raised her right arm and—*ooff*—shoved Lucie. And it wasn't a light shove either. The force propelled Lucie backward, sent her stumbling as she reached out, finding nothing to grab on to for balance. *Dang it.* Why did she have to be the one everyone got to literally push around. Anticipating the crash, she stretched her arms behind her and steeled herself. One, two, three—*whack!* She slammed into the wall, the back of her skull taking a direct hit.

"Ow!"

Pain shot in all directions and the beige walls blurred, everything swaying while Lucie's stomach pitched.

Anna.

Lucie blinked. *Blink-blink, blink-blink.* Her vision cleared enough to see Anna turning away, rushing to the back door.

Oh, no you don't.

If Anna got away, Lucie might never be cleared. Shaking off the dizziness, she exploded into a sprint straight at the leggy blonde.

Lucie latched onto the briefcase, tugging on it as Anna shoved at her.

"Hey," Anna said, "let go. Are you crazy?"

"Crazy? Please. I'm borderline psychotic right now."

Anna shoved her again. *That's it. I'm done.* Lucie let out a growl—a really mean one.

"Shove me again and you're cooked."

Then she spun and jumped, landing on Anna's back.

"Whoa. Get off me!"

Nope. *No can do.* Lucie lifted her legs and locked them around Anna's waist. The woman teetered on her heels and sent the two of them careening into the wall. A burst of air shot from Lucie's lungs, but she hung on as Anna lined her up for another slam.

"Lucie!"

Joey's voice. From the front entrance. She swiveled her head, found her brother and Tim with a uniformed cop.

"Get her off me," Anna cried.

"Luce," Tim said, "off!"

How many times had he said *that* to her in the last six months?

Joey and Tim rushed toward them, each taking a side and blocking the exits.

"She's nuts," Anna said. "She attacked me. I'm pressing charges."

Lucie hopped off Anna just as Dad opened the door. "SWAT is here."

SWAT? Dear God.

But Lucie didn't care about all that. All she wanted to hear was that they'd nabbed Beanie Boy. "Did you get him?"

"Yeah. He's locked in the back of a squad car." Tim grinned at Anna. "Singing like a bird."

Finally, they'd know who the heck plotted this blackmail scenario. "Who is he? Tell me he and Anna are partners."

"Better. He's her brother."

Her...what?

Lucie curled her fingers into fists, visualized all her anger flowing into those fists. Oh, she should take a shot. Just one good punch. She narrowed her eyes at Anna. "Your brother. Soooo, evil."

"Yep," Tim said. "According to him, Anna saw the safe open. After she and Molly left, they spent a few minutes on the sidewalk talking and parted ways. By then, the fire had broken out. Luce, Anna saw you come out the back and figured the door was still unlocked. She slipped upstairs into Antoine's office and helped herself to the recipe. She figured the fire was a convenient distraction."

"And we didn't even see her."

Tim shrugged. "Everyone was outside by then."

Curt the negotiator entered via the back door with Molly in tow. Lucie jabbed her finger at Anna. "The guy with the backpack is her brother. All this time your assistant was behind it. And you accused me!"

Tim set his big hand on Lucie's shoulder. "Calm down. The brother said it was Anna's idea. They set Molly up."

Now Molly whirled on Anna. "*What?* After everything I've done for you? I gave you a fucking career."

F-bombs. *You go, girl.*

"You *gave* me?" Anna scoffed. "Please. I've been slave labor for two years."

"You were in training. What did you expect?"

Anna swung to Lucie, her eyes like two machetes, ready to carve someone to pieces. "I've been the grunt. Begging her for more responsibility. All I wanted was a client of my own. I worked and worked, and all she'd give me was menial tasks."

Lucie held up a finger. "Hey, I take exception to that. She gave you the Coco Barknell contract to handle for Antoine."

"Yeah," Molly said. "Did you want me to just hand you a hundred-million dollar contract? You start small and work your way up. Like I did."

But Anna didn't want to hear it. She shook her head and turned her fiery eyes back to Molly. "I was ready for more."

"You're ready when I say you're ready. For fuck's sake, how was framing me going to get you a promotion?"

Yowzer. This woman made Ro look like Shirley Temple.

"You'd be gone," Tim said.

All eyes went to him and he held up his hands. "She planted the recipe in Molly's office, then set up the cash drop. My guess is she planned on leaving that two mil somewhere that would implicate you. Does she have access to your business accounts?"

Molly's face stretched into a mass of disbelief. "She has the account numbers. She's not a signer."

Huh. This girl should work for Dad with that scheming, delinquent mind.

"Wow." Lucie faced Anna. "You thought you could set up Molly then slide right in and take over her clients when she went to jail. Aren't you something else?"

For a brief second, Lucie stood quietly, absorbing the idea that this girl, clearly lonely and in constant need of approval, plotted against a woman who'd entrusted her with her business.

"All I wanted," Anna said, "was a little responsibility. Something to take care of. I'm good at taking care of things."

Lucie let out a long sigh. "Not anymore you're not."

15

Two days later, Lucie sat in Antoine's conference room listening as Tim laid out the case against Annalise.

Lucie stared out the window at the blackening winter sky. Nothing about this situation felt right.

At the head of the table, Antoine remained stoic, seemingly embalmed over the fact that someone on his team had tried to swindle him. Any reaction to his manager/girlfriend's assistant almost ruining him was hidden beneath stony cheeks and a focused gaze. A facade of nothingness. Molly sat across from Lucie, her ever-present leather portfolio in front of her. Did she feel responsible? It was, after all, her employee who'd created this mess.

Proof that it happened to the best of them. Even a woman with a law degree.

"As of this morning," Tim said, "Anna is facing a slew of charges. Extortion, conspiracy, possibly trademark infringement, the works. Lucie decided to give her a break and not press charges."

Antoine met her gaze. "After what she—*we*—put you through, that was kind."

Recognizing that, Lucie nodded. "She's a disturbed young woman. I don't see how another five years in jail will help what ails her. She needs help."

Antoine ran a hand over his face. "I just don't get why she did it."

Tim sat back in his chair, his big shoulders relaxing into the soft leather. Still in his suit, but with the tie gone and the top button on his shirt undone, he looked so darned handsome Lucie's heart thumped. Her man. Right there with her.

"Her lawyer," Tim said, "had a psych evaluation done. According to them, she suffers from Rescuer Syndrome."

"Rescuer Syndrome?"

"It's when someone feels an overwhelming need to rescue people. In whatever way possible."

Antoine let out a derisive grunt. "How does blackmail equal rescuing me?"

The two-million-dollar question. And somehow, Lucie thought she knew the answer. Understood on an emotional level most wouldn't. Sometimes it took a mob boss's kid to get into the basement of those emotions.

"I had a conversation with her the other day," Lucie said. "Her father died when she was young. Her mother never recovered emotionally and Anna became responsible for her brother. It sounds as if she did most of the parenting."

"Which," Tim said, "is why he went along with her crazy scheme. He's been beholden to her. All these years. And she played on that to fulfill her own needs. According to the shrink, with Anna, it's an endless cycle. She needs to feel needed. If she doesn't, she's left thinking about her own issues and that sends her into a downward spiral."

Molly held out a hand. "So, as long as she's rescuing people, she feels good."

Now Lucie faced Molly, a woman so used to being in

charge she'd forgotten how to listen when the people around her spoke. "Yes. Except she wanted Antoine."

The chef's eyes shot wide. "Come again?"

"Not in the physical sense. She wanted you as her client. Someone she could focus on and not have to share with Molly."

"Well," Molly said, "*that* wasn't happening. She wasn't nearly ready."

Tim shrugged. "Guessing she knew that. She's been trying to come up with a way to get the recipe. For months she'd been planning. She just couldn't get around the security to the actual recipe. She got lucky when the fire broke out. Then, hoping to keep heat on Lucie, she had her brother break into Lucie's car and plant a copy of the recipe in her briefcase. That bought her a fallback in case framing Molly didn't work. And here we are." He made eye contact with Molly. "By framing you, she thought she'd slide into your chair. She'd assure your clients she could handle their business and she'd take over."

Antoine leaned in and propped his elbows on the table. "Her plan was to rescue me by saving the day after Molly went down."

"Pretty much," Tim said.

"That's...calculated." He swiveled to Molly. "Guess we need to vet your employees better."

For once, the woman stayed silent. All of this landed squarely in her lap.

Antoine scrubbed his hands over his face and up into his hair. For the first time, Lucie noted the shadows under his eyes. Who knew when he'd slept last.

A gust of wind rattled the windowpane. Lucie glanced over, thankful for the distraction. At this point, she had nothing to say. They'd accused her of horrible things. And tried to sue her.

"Lucie," Antoine said, bringing her attention back to him. "I'm sorry." He gestured to Molly. "We both are."

Finally, Molly nodded. "I *am* sorry, Lucie. No matter how I looked at it, I always came up with you being the one."

"I was the obvious one. Still, it wasn't fun being accused of something like that."

"Which is why," Antoine said, "we'd like to make it up to you."

Now we're talking. "I hope you're dropping this lawsuit."

"Yes. That was a scare tactic."

Well, it worked. "Thank you." She slid an envelope from her messenger bag. "This is the copy of the recipe Anna planted in my bag. I haven't made any copies."

Antoine held the envelope up. "Thank you. That's... really generous after what we accused you of."

"I'm not a crook. I make my own way."

He set the envelope on the table, staring at it for a few long seconds before he met her gaze again. "We'd like to hire you back. Brie misses her walks with Lauren."

If she had it in her, Lucie could take a stand here. Be the insulted, humiliated party and tell Antoine to shove his dog-walking gig where the sun don't shine.

If she had it in her.

The truth was, she couldn't blame him for assuming she'd been the blackmailer. After talking it over with Tim, dissecting this thing five hundred different ways, she'd have come to the same conclusion.

Means, motive, opportunity.

She'd had all three.

"I'd appreciate that," Lucie said. "It's important for us to keep our customers happy." She smiled. "Even the four-legged ones."

Antoine waggled his fingers at Molly and she retrieved a folder from the portfolio.

He slid the folder to Lucie. She eyeballed it. "What is it?"

"A contract. The dog food. We have some details to work out—and I want to meet the woman who created it—but if it all checks out, I'll do it."

The dog food deal. *Yes!* Later, she'd do a happy dance. Right now? She needed to be a tough, hard-as-nails businesswoman. One who wouldn't get screwed, as Dad would say.

Previously, she'd floated a 50/50 partnership and Antoine balked. After this ordeal, she wouldn't take less. If she had to, she'd walk away and find another partner. Simply on principle. Did that make her stubborn and prideful?

Yes.

She didn't care. She knew her worth.

She glanced at Tim, who wore his detective poker face. No help there. At least not yet. She flipped the file open, perusing the contract until the legalese made her head spin. She skipped to the paragraph outlining the terms of the deal.

$500,000 in capital from Antoine. No salary for Lucie or Jo-Jo and...

A 50/50 split.

He'd given her exactly what she'd asked for. Lucie kept her posture intact, no collapsing into relieved giggles. Refusing to react, she continued reading. Pretended to anyway. After seeing that 50/50, everything went to mush.

She paused another minute or so, flipping through

pages of the contract, but not really absorbing anything. Her lawyer would have to read it anyway.

Antoine held his palm up. "I gave you the deal you asked for."

"I see that. Thank you. I know it's a good faith gesture on your part. I appreciate it."

"Is that a yes?"

"I'll need to talk to Jo-Jo and Ro—she's a partner in Coco Barknell. If they agree, I'd say you have a deal."

By eight o'clock, the lights still blazed in Coco Barknell.

Ro stood behind her desk, her librarian glasses perched on the end of her nose. She flipped her long, sable hair over her shoulder then did a little wiggle as she adjusted her skirt. Even at the end of the day, in silly glasses, she could be a movie star.

Ro shoved her laptop and the folder with the dog food contract into her briefcase. She'd yet to say anything—not one thing—after reading the terms of the deal.

Four times.

All while Lucie patiently waited, busying herself answering emails. Tim, bless his patience, sat with his feet on their conference table, tossing Lucie's rubber stress ball in the air. Toss, catch, toss, catch, toss, catch. Over and over again.

He'd do that all night if she let him. Men. Such simple creatures.

Ro zipped her briefcase closed and removed her glasses, waving them in the air like some big-shot CEO addressing her minions. "You really want to do this food deal?"

"I do. It wouldn't kill us to diversify. And it's a good deal."

The front door swung open. Joey stepped in, bringing a blast of cold air with him. "Hey," he said. "Let's go. I'm hungry."

Ro held her briefcase out for Joey to carry. "Relax, ape man."

Tim snorted a laugh.

After taking the briefcase, Joey smacked Ro on the ass and kissed her. "You're funny."

Romance. Joey style.

On her way to the door, Ro paused and turned back. "Make the deal, Luce. What the hell. We can do anything together."

A burst of something bright and loud and...awesome pinged around inside Lucie. She threw her hands in the air. "Whoot! Thank you. This will be great. You'll see. I promise."

She'd gone from being accused of theft and blackmail to owning a dog food company. Not bad.

As Ro and Joey strode out, Lucie hopped up, charging Tim and snatching the stress ball from mid-air. She leaned over and hit him with a toe-curling lip lock that included her tongue. A lot of her tongue.

A lot of his tongue, too.

With Tim, all her inhibitions vanished. He had that way about him. Acceptance. A casual understanding that boosted her confidence.

She wrapped her hand around the back of his head, holding him there while she mauled him. With the lights on and anyone on the street watching.

Who cared?

She loved him.

He let out a low groan and nipped at her bottom lip. "I guess you're happy."

Oh, she was happy all right. She stood tall, ran the back of her hand over his cheek. Such a good man. "I am indeed. Tired, but happy."

"Good. You ready for dinner? We'll celebrate. Anywhere you want to go. Then I'm taking you to my place and screwing your lights out."

Ha. "You're on, mister."

She turned, ready to head back to her desk. The blackness beyond the shop window stopped her. Another cold Chicago night. She paused, steeling her weary bones for the cold.

What she needed was warmth. Days of it. And rest. For months she'd been pushing hard, building the business, forcing her brain to multi-task in more ways than she could count.

She faced Tim again. "You know where I really want to go?"

"Where?"

"On vacation. With you."

A smile lit his face. "Yeah?"

"Yep. Someplace warm." She gestured to the front windows. "Get us out of this miserable cold. Plus, I'm tired."

He set his feet on the floor, anchoring the swivel chair, and drew her onto his lap. "It's been a wild few months."

"It sure has. What do you say, handsome? Do you have any vacation time coming?"

"I do. And I have an uncle in Florida I haven't seen in a couple years. How about we make a pit-stop at his place and then head to the Keys?"

The Keys. Oh, that sounded...amazing. Lucie had never been, but for years dreamed of cruising the causeways in a convertible. Warm sun and ocean air. Perfect way to zap stress.

She nodded. "I'd love that. I'll research places to stay. Maybe we can find a beach cottage. Just the two of us."

He patted her on the upper part of her rear. "Honey, you and me. Alone? That makes me the luckiest guy alive."

She leaned in, kissed him again then drew back. "I think it makes me the luckiest *girl* alive. You and me. Tim and Lucie."

Just like they'd agreed. No mob princess. No Chicago PD detective. Just Lucie and Tim.

And Lucie couldn't find a whole lot wrong with that.

A NOTE TO READERS

Dear reader,

Thank you for reading *Cooked.* I hope you enjoyed it. If you did, please help others find it by sharing it with friends on social media and writing a review.

Sharing the book with your friends and leaving a review helps other readers decide to take the plunge into the nutty world of Lucie Rizzo. So please consider taking a moment to tell your friends how much you enjoyed the story. Even a few words expressing what you enjoyed most about the story is a huge help. Thank you!

Happy reading!
Adrienne

ACKNOWLEDGMENTS

Many thanks to my readers for all the emails and social media posts regarding Lucie and the gang. I am in awe and so grateful for your support. Muhwah!

Speaking of my readers, a very special thank you to Jan Limp and Pam Howell for helping me name Chef Rueben LeBeau. The name was perfect! Thank you also to my dear friends Kevin and Cindy Palmer and Mara, John and Josh Leach for allowing me to use their beloved dogs in my books. You guys are awesome!

Thanks also to Jon Flaute for sharing your knowledge about the finance world. I learn something new with every book and I'm always amazed at the wealth of information people are so generous with.

A giant thank you to Misty Evans and Tracey Devlyn for keeping me sane during the writing of this book. As with any job, some projects are more challenging than others. This one falls in the challenging column, but I'm lucky enough to have friends that help me clean up my messes.

As usual, thanks to my guys for making me smile every day. I love you.

ABOUT THE AUTHOR

 **Adrienne Giordano** is a *USA Today* bestselling author of over twenty romantic suspense and mystery novels. She is a Jersey girl at heart, but now lives in the Midwest with her workaholic husband, sports-obsessed son and Buddy the Wheaten Terrorist (Terrier). She is a cofounder of Romance University blog and Lady Jane's Salon-Naperville, a reading series dedicated to romantic fiction.

For more information on Adrienne, including her Internet haunts, contest updates, and details on her upcoming novels, please visit her at:

www.AdrienneGiordano.com
agiordano@adriennegiordano.com